To E
from the

GW00854239

FOR THE LOVE OF DOG

R R

R ADICAL R OONEY

authorHOUSE®

(FINISHED COPY)

AuthorHouse™ UK
1663 Liberty Drive
Bloomington, IN 47403 USA
www.authorhouse.co.uk
Phone: 0800.197.4150

Published by AuthorHouse 01/26/2017

ISBN: 978-1-5049-9438-5 (sc)
ISBN: 978-1-5049-9439-2 (e)

Library of Congress Control Number: 2015919644

Print information available on the last page.

DEDICATION

*For the Animal Kingdom, which suffers
so greatly at the hands of man.*

ACKNOWLEDGEMENTS

L214.com
Greenpeace
Mother Earth
Friends of the Earth
Sir Paul McCartney
P.E.T.A.
Elim Missions
Quarr Abbey
Darvel Community
World Animal Protection
animalsaviours.org
The Nonhuman Rights Project
British Union for the Abolition of Vivisection
Cruelty-Free International
Dr Pearsall PhD. Nexus Magazine
Royal Society for the Prevention of Cruelty to Animals

KIRKUS REVIEW

In the first novel from Rooney (*A Year on the Streets*, 2012),
a Chinese immigrant's life in England is transformed
through religion and a deep connection with animals he
once unthinkingly persecuted.

Rooney, a Northern Irish poet whose previous book
explored homelessness in his adopted hometown of
Hastings, England, turns to animal rights. Three illegal
immigrants who work in a restaurant in London's
Chinatown are arrested for smuggling opium and
slaughtering dogs for meat. Ping is the ringleader, with
Lee Fong Chu and La-Lu Wing as his accomplices. The
others are jailed, but Lee gets off lightly and emerges
as the protagonist. He moves to Hastings, where after
some time squatting and abusing alcohol, he finds work
as a hotel night porter. Blamed for a theft, he too ends
up in prison, where he has an explosive reunion with
Ping. Freed again, he unexpectedly turns into an animal
lover when he adopts a deceased neighbour's schnauzer,
takes up horseback riding, and falls in with animal rights
activists. Meanwhile, La-Lu, having kicked her heroin
addiction and become a Christian, will trade prison for a
cloister. Lee, too, comes to believe in God but not before

exacting brutal vigilante justice on animal abusers in both England and China.

Despite the book's surprisingly high body count for a short novel, (282 Pages) it's stuffed with plot, and the turns are often sudden and melodramatic. The portrait of Lee is fairly nuanced; nevertheless, it can be hard to believe that a man who once skinned live dogs would later commit murder to avenge animal suffering. Still, the novel's sentiments are genuine and its message important: "we are all animals but rational animals, waging a constant dialogue with our environment and our Creator."

Contents

ACKNOWLEDGEMENTS v

KIRKUS REVIEW vii

INTRODUCTION xi

CHAPTER ONE 1

CHAPTER TWO 15

CHAPTER THREE 33

CHAPTER FOUR 46

CHAPTER FIVE 70

CHAPTER SIX 81

CHAPTER SEVEN 99

CHAPTER EIGHT 109

CHAPTER NINE 134

CHAPTER TEN 162

CHAPTER ELEVEN 177

CHAPTER TWELVE 189

CHAPTER THIRTEEN 206

CHAPTER FOURTEEN 218

CHAPTER FIFTEEN 231

CHAPTER SIXTEEN 239

CHAPTER SEVENTEEN 254

AUTHORS PAGE 267

INTRODUCTION

It was headline news; at least in all the tabloids. A homeless woman, wandering the streets of London had been rummaging through the bins of a prestigious restaurant, in the heart of Chinatown, when she discovered a very large bone. Thinking it might be human she pointed it out to a passing street warden who called in the authorities.

In the event, it turned out to be a large animal bone, but Trading Standards were intrigued to know what sort of animal was being prepared for public consumption, and instigated an enquiry. The premises were searched and some anomalies discovered; there were carcasses of dead dogs stowed in freezers and various pelts stashed about the premises. Two starving dogs were also found chained up in the cellar.

In the search, certain packages were seized by forensics, and found to contain copious amounts of pure opium. Three suspects were taken into custody and charged with numerous offences. The case involved Health and Safety personnel, the local council, the Drug Squad and also the Royal Society for the Prevention of Cruelty to Animals.

Three Chinese immigrants were charged; two men and a woman. It transpired during their bail hearing that all three had been brought up in an orphanage in Mainland China and had entered the country illegally. The ringleader, one Ping Hey Mung, was suspected of running a drug cartel in Chinatown, which garnered huge amounts of money. He was a distinctive individual of huge build; not tall but very stocky with massive crab-like arms and a huge head, seemingly planted onto his shoulders. When he entered a room his bulk preceded him like a garland of pride, but Ping Hey Mung was tough, in the way some men like to think they are, for he had no fear of man or beast. He was not short of money either, and had developed expensive tastes for fast cars and women.

He owned a number of properties including the restaurant, a house in Chinatown, which he rented out to his Chinese workers, and a bungalow by the sea. He also possessed a formidable reputation and many enemies.

The other man, Lee Fong Chu, had been a lifelong friend but was as different to him as chalk to cheese. He looked like life had mauled him, leaving memories etched in the craggy confines of his wrinkled face. Lee Fong was a simple soul who never much liked himself, finding it difficult to relate to others. His hobby was making large kites, and his only other pastime was the practice of match building, where he would cut the heads off matches to construct ornate little buildings. He spent many hours making them, and sometimes managed to sell them to customers in the restaurant.

On Chinese New Year he would convert the match-heads into firecrackers to sell on the streets, but realised years ago he would never get rich, like his friend Ping Hey, and although he dreamt of marriage realised he was in no position to consider this. His only friends were his co-defendants, Ping Hey Mung and La-Lu Wing.

La-Lu, on the other hand, had always loved Lee Fong but kept her feelings secret because she had acquired certain tastes in life, namely an addiction to opium and an expensive lifestyle, catered for by her drug smuggling. Being strikingly beautiful enabled her to escape certain situations, which unfortunately had now caught up with her, but she was now prepared to accept the consequences of her actions.

CHAPTER ONE

Despite the promise of Spring, shards of frost still clung to the ornate spires of the Old Bailey. Through the hallowed corridors of the High Court, a host of ushers guided people to their seats.

'Come to Order,' cried an usher, as the public gallery settled down and various participants took their places. 'All rise!' called the clerk of the court. The Court all stood as the judge stalked in, resplendent in his ermine, cloak and wig. He felt these lent him a certain gravitas, sadly lacking by the rest of the court, who were limited to more mundane attire.

As the judge took his seat, the clerk announced, 'Court in session', enabling the ensemble of lawyers, barristers and jurors to assert their presence with a flamboyant rustling of papers, and clearing of throats.

The Press, representing media from around the world, had spilled with vulturous intent from the crowded Press Box into the confines of the public gallery.

In a more strident tone, the usher then declared, 'Silence in court', causing the cacophony of chatter and rustlings to cease, save for a few random coughs and a muffled buzz from the public gallery, making him repeat his demand, whereupon silence finally reigned.

This, reflected the judge, is a rather serious case with far-reaching and potentially political repercussions. It involved opium and heroin worth millions, being smuggled from Mainland China over a period of years, with numerous charges of animal cruelty involved and even the poisoning of some members of the public.

The judge himself was an animal lover but not a man renowned for his sense of humour or ebullience. Even in private, residing at leisure in his country manor, his good wife found his demeanour, at best, taciturn.

High Court judges usually acquire certain virtues as they move up the hierarchy of the judiciary; infinite patience, impregnable character and the discernment of a sage. Coupled with decades of experience and a regal resolve, he was a formidable foe for any criminal. Even in atmospheres of confusion and mendacity, his rulings were always resolute and crystal clear, curbed with impartial advice, redolent of wisdom.

The three defendants were called to the dock to enter their pleas, which was the only time they would appear together, except when the verdicts were announced.

The dock surrounded a set of concrete steps leading down to the holding cells; it was chest high and a buttress of spiked rails deterred any escape. The three Chinese defendants stood flanked by prison guards who proceeded to remove their handcuffs.

They blinked in confusion, as they suddenly found themselves in the middle of a massively orchestrated theatre, and realised they were now centre-stage.

One by one they placed their right hands on a Bible and were sworn in. 'This is risible,' thought the judge, 'all three have sworn oaths on the Bible, but they've never heard of it before.' He decided to explain to them that this oath consisted of telling the truth, the whole truth, and nothing but the truth, and that anything less would be considered 'perjury' and they could still go to prison even if found innocent.

His profound gaze rested on the trio; a pair of men, about thirty, flanked by a tall elegantly dressed woman in her late twenties. They were all, he learned, illegal immigrants although one of them, Ping Hey Mung, had been running a restaurant in the heart of Chinatown.

If this lot is found guilty, reflected the judge, I shall recommend deportation, after time served. He thought one of the men, Lee Fong, had a contrite air about him, and looked remorseful. The judge took a moment to study him.

With some people great sadness can be seen in their eyes, and Lee Fong was such a person. The eyes mirror the soul, the judge mused, but looking at his blank stare devoid of emotion, the judge concluded this poor reprobate doesn't appear to have much soul. He looks rather dispassionate, and usually this means he is either unaware of his predicament, or imagines he is innocent. The judge then studied Ping Hey Mung. This one looks devious and cunning, and I suspect he's the ringleader.

The judge observed Ping Hey looking furtively round the court, without moving his stocky head, searching for anyone who could possibly implicate him. As the judge expected, the two men pleaded 'not guilty' to charges of possession and distribution of a class 'A' drug, namely heroin, which had been smuggled into the country by the woman, La-Lu. She also pleaded not guilty to these charges, as well as numerous counts of illegal importation. The judge noted that La-Lu had an air of confidence, which suggested she did not scare easily. Although Chinese, her eyes did not betray her ethnicity unless, considered the judge, she had indulged in some of that popular surgery so many of her people tried, in efforts to straighten their eyes. She did look Westernized, with demure suit and long dark hair, coiffured above impeccable makeup. He tried to catch her eye but she never seemed to look directly at him.

A sign of guilt, he surmised. He noted she possessed the high cheekbones of classic beauty, and sported petite firm breasts, which stood proud on her slender figure, enhancing her slim waist and wide hips. He decided that she was certainly the most attractive woman in Court and made a mental note not to let his judgment be clouded by her obvious beauty.

She and Ping Hey had their own barristers, who were Queens Counsellors, and the judge was fully aware of the exorbitant expense involved in such a defence. He noted that Lee Fong could not afford a Q.C., but had been granted Legal Aid for a court appointed lawyer.

The two men also faced further charges of theft, animal cruelty, and public health endangerment. The judge was not amused by the animal cruelty charges, which involved the theft and killing of a number of dogs. His favourite pastime was 'riding to hounds' and he loved dogs, especially his old Doberman, which he often paraded round his estate but which had recently gone missing.

As the case progressed, the prosecution set out to prove Ping Hey's modus operandi, in conducting a restaurant business as a cover for supplying packages of heroin to clientele via take-away meals, which Lee Fong delivered on his little moped.

The prosecution told the jury that La-Lu was just a common 'drug-mule', secreting heroin inside her body. Apparently, she had made frequent trips from China using a number of false passports, but the jury laughed when told that she used her frequent-flyer points to purchase electronic kitchen scales to weigh out the packets of heroin. The jury then heard the prosecution claim that these were passed to Ping Hey, who now admitted that although he knew about the drugs, he thought she had acquired them locally, with no smuggling ever involved. The judge doubted this, for the trio had known each other since childhood, when they were all reared in the same orphanage in Mainland China, so it was unlikely she would have kept news of her trips back home a secret from her comrades. He listened when it was explained how the pure heroin was 'stepped on' by Ping Hey who diluted it with Novocaine, a dental anaesthetic, before getting his simple-minded cohort, Lee Fong, to distribute it around Chinatown.

Ping Hey claimed that Lee Fong knew the meals held packets of heroin, because he and La-Lu had organised it all between themselves. Ping claimed he suspected what they were up to but was powerless to stop them, for fear of alienating his clientele who would probably boycott the restaurant.

He claimed Lee and La-Lu never shared their ill-gotten gains with him, and begged the Courts indulgence for having allowed his premises to be used for such deplorable practices; he then swore he had never touched the stuff in his whole life, which drew a ripple of amusement from the public gallery.

Unfortunately for him Customs and Excise were involved in the case and were able to enlighten the Court as to the various assets held by Ping Hey.

Apparently, not only did he own the restaurant but also a house in Chinatown, which he rented out to Chinese workers, one of whom was Lee Fong. He had also purchased a bungalow by the seaside in St. Leonards, near Hastings and paid cash for a new Mercedes sports car, to complement his four-by-four, which DNA analysis proved was the vehicle used for transporting the dogs that were stolen.

The judge pondered these discrepancies until he remembered the cruelty charges. 'Can you clarify the other charges?' he asked the prosecution.

'Certainly, Your Worship,' came the reply. 'It would appear that these two men would drive out of town to a remote park near Hastings where they would kidnap a large dog, bundle it into the 'four by four' vehicle for the trip back to London and keep it in the cellar beneath their restaurant, until needed.'

'Until needed?' queried the judge, conjuring a tone of naïve innocence.

'Well, Your Worship,' continued the prosecution, 'if the men could not seize a stray dog near to their place of work, they would acquire one farther afield, and store it in the cellar under their restaurant to fatten it up.'

'For what purpose?' the judge asked. The prosecution is really labouring this point, he mused.

The prosecution then dropped their bombshell. 'The dogs would be skinned alive, then beaten with baseball bats until dead, to ensure their flesh was full of adrenalin; after which they were fed to the public in the restaurant.'

At this point a lady juror fainted. The judge decided to call a recess and Court was adjourned. The Press stormed out, grappling for their mobiles.

The judge retired to Chambers, where a snack of paté-de-fois-gras and biscuits were served him. The judge considered himself an erudite man of taste, yet he was blissfully unaware of the techniques employed to garner this paté. He was an animal lover, but had no qualms about eating animals.

He knew this expensive delicacy was actually the diseased liver of a goose, but had never considered the methods employed to harvest it.

He might have been put off by learning that the geese in question are subjected to horrific tortures in its production, where some would even have their webbed feet stapled to a wooden floor. Most would be imprisoned all their lives in long rows of metal cages; unable to turn around or move about. These cages would all be stacked together, facing forward, to simplify the feeding process. A metal pipe would then be rammed down their throats, to force-feed them three pounds of food every day; equivalent to a human eating forty-five pounds of pasta, at one sitting.

Sometimes their wings are broken and their beaks wired so they can't expel the surplus. Because of all this, their livers get diseased, and swell to ten times their normal size. When their throats get so damaged with gashes from the pipes, these are punched directly into their gullets. In a month or so, they are so fat they cannot move, leaving them prey to rats that gnaw at their festering wounds, as they wallow in their own waste. Most will be very lucky if they survive twelve weeks. They live in such agony that they often tear out their own feathers; but even if they don't their chests are stripped bare, when all these feathers are cruelly ripped out to make goose-down pillows; this leaves them bleeding and in pain. To stem this bleeding their wounds are then stitched up, without any anaesthetic.

The Judge thought he was aware of most foreign tastes, but never fathomed the extent of the culinary expertise which had just graced his table.

He had just indulged in a portion of Royal-Beluga caviar, when he suddenly remembered that his wife had taken him some years ago to this very restaurant to celebrate their anniversary. He became incensed, for he now realised he may have actually consumed dog-meat. The fact that his faithful old Doberman had gone missing did nothing to enhance his current disposition.

He now recalled how the Court was told the dogs' pelts were later sold to a local Chinese furrier, who fashioned them into muffs, collars and gloves. This reprobate was also arrested, but making a mental note to check the labelling on his wife's fur-stole, he relished the imminent trial of this unusual furrier.

Meanwhile, down in the holding cells, the three defendants had time to reflect on the day's events, as each in turn gave evidence. Ping Hey wondered about the sensibilities of an English jury and muttered to himself, 'If they think the way we kill dogs in England is bad, they should see how we kill them in China; or how we serve monkeys at dinner parties.'

Reality now hit Lee Fong like a sudden chill, as he sensed the irony of this situation, where they were all once again incarcerated together.

'This could even be worse than the orphanage,' thought Lee. He recalled his escape from there, with Ping Hey, many years previously. He remembered all the years of hard work and sacrifice he had to endure in the Chinese dog markets, to buy his own little shack, only to have it demolished for the Beijing Olympics. He had received some compensation for his loss and felt fortunate, because many of his neighbours got nothing. He was resourceful enough to save some money for his escape to Europe, some years later, when he was eventually reunited with his old friend in London, Ping Hey, who offered him a home and a job for which he remained very grateful.

Then he thought of La-Lu, whom he had secretly loved and desired for years. She had also been confined in the orphanage, until she became of age on her fifteenth birthday, but he had escaped with Ping, when she was only twelve years old. It was only when they met years later, in the meat markets, that he really became infatuated with her. She had been released into the care of some distant relatives who were too overworked and poverty-stricken to be bothered by her and because of her Western looks, had led a lonely life.

Most of the villagers ostracized her; it was common knowledge that her father had come to China from the West, as a missionary, but had abandoned her before his return home.

She was taller than most of the girls in the orphanage, with a subtle blend of fine features that were not an asset in that institution, for she soon learnt her main role was to be subservient to the custodians, men or women, in every way imaginable.

Lee remembered how the adults, who were supposed to be guarding them, would drag the girls off in the middle of the night. The boys slept in separate dormitories to the girls, but could hear their screams echo in the dark of night.

The boys would interrogate the girls in the light of day, but none of the tear-stained victims offered any details. The boys' imaginations took over where their knowledge ceased and fevered horrors coursed through their minds, scarring them forever.

Lee then remembered how the girls behaved afterwards; they never spoke much, and never looked you in the eye: they also seemed to wash themselves a lot of the time. He remembered how some of these girls would walk around as though in a trance, never paying attention to their looks, and with scant regard for the heat of the sun. They were easy to spot because they quickly grew emaciated and seemed very careless, frequently cutting themselves for some reason or other.

Within a few months most of them took their own lives, and nobody ever mentioned them again. It was the way of the world, thought Lee, and he was glad to be a boy.

La-Lu, on the other hand, seemed different. She was sad to be a girl and never smiled much, but managed to survive for she knew and accepted the fact that the male species ruled that orphanage, and that in China many of her sex were killed at birth. Her one childish dream was to get away, marry someone rich and have children of her own but she realised on reaching puberty that she was not ovulating and was probably infertile. She reasoned that the constant sexual abuse was to blame, but resolved to tell no one, though it constantly preyed on her mind. Her grim past had gifted her with the patience and perseverance she now needed, in the face of adversity.

Lee Fong thought of her now, as he realised she would once again be locked up at the mercy of others, probably to be abused again, and he wept.

But at least she had lived in the world a while, and had travelled, and seen things of which he only dreamed. He had always wanted to marry La-Lu, but never had the courage to ask for he sensed she saw him as just a loser with no prospects. He felt she viewed him as some sort of inferior being; he certainly felt inferior for he had developed a limp as a result of a bad beating at the orphanage and suffered from asthma attacks, which frequently proved debilitating. His back was also giving trouble, for he was prone to severe spasms, which were unendurably painful. Being an illegal alien meant he could not seek medical advice and had to rely on the numbing qualities of Ping's opium to alleviate the pain.

Ping Hey sat alone in his cell thinking of his old friend, whom he first met in the orphanage when he was ten years old. Lee was only nine, but they had known each other ever since.

'Twenty years is a long time,' he thought. He remembered first meeting this simple kid who looked up to him and called him 'cousin'. They would sometimes talk with La-Lu, but she was younger, and never had much to say.

Ping was much stronger and smarter than Lee but took him under his wing protecting him from the bullies, who had once beaten him badly, breaking his leg. Ping even taught him how to steal food from the others, and how to get extra, by pretending to be sick.

They provided each other with solace and secrets in the seclusion of their hostile home. One day, Ping decided he would never go hungry again; that he would escape and always have lots of food to eat and enough to feed others, like Lee. He would like that and, perhaps someday, might even make a living from it.

By the time he was eleven, he had planned their great escape. He took Lee into his confidence and they swore secrecy to each other, not telling any of the others. When they left, they said goodbye to no one, except La-Lu.

Ping remembered the night they got into the van, where the weekly laundry was stacked for collection. Some bags lay ready in the back so they climbed inside and found two with enough space for each of them to snuggle inside, but were nearly suffocated when other bags were piled on top of them in the morning.

However, as soon as they sensed the van leaving the compound, Ping managed to escape from his bag and release Lee. Thinking back, he now wished he had left him behind.

Although the incident occurred many years ago it stayed fresh in his mind, like the time he smuggled himself as a young man across Europe, hiding for days without food, beside the Channel Tunnel in France.

He ran in the dark with scores of others to clamber beneath the night train bound for London, and had to hang on desperately as the monster thundered beneath the sea, ploughing a path to freedom. The Gendarmerie ignored the hordes of refugees as they scurried alongside the electric rails, because if they successfully jumped the train they were no longer France's problem, and if they got run over or electrocuted they were no longer France's problem.

So without a penny and speaking only Mandarin he managed to find his way to Chinatown, where an enigmatic old man befriended him, after he begged for food at his take-away restaurant.

Ping then thought of the old man with the long white beard who always seemed a comforting sight, beetling about his business, bent almost double. Because Ping was so strong he was soon able to take over most of the chores, even shutting up shop at midnight, when he was then allowed to sleep in the cellar. When the old boy died years later, he left his little business to Ping, who slowly built it up over the years.

When they escaped the orphanage, Lee Fong went to work in the nearby 'dog village' while Ping escaped to the West. Although they kept in touch, Lee felt he would never see his old friend again. However, an opportunity arose when La-Lu also escaped to the West and came to work for Ping in Chinatown, in London. They made elaborate plans to build up a smuggling racket and decided they could use Lee in their setup. Lee was immensely grateful to his old friends, who sent him a false passport and extra funds to get to London. Leaving the noise and stench of the dog market was like being resurrected into another world.

CHAPTER TWO

In the adjacent cell, Lee was thinking of his old friend Ping, who had so often saved his skin in the orphanage. He smiled as he recalled their friendship, remembering how Ping showed him how to dry out tea-leaves so they could be re-used and how to roll cigarettes almost thinner than the matches used to light them.

He had not realised until now, that Ping had merely used him as his personal slave, when he first arrived in London, getting him to do his dirty work.

He found that Ping hoarded everything; even old clothes, which he grew out of, would never be thrown away. Lee thought Ping was the meanest and greediest person he'd ever met, but he put this down to the deprivation they had all endured as children.

Yet, I never acted like that, he reflected. Ping still preferred to sleep in the cellar even when the old man offered them cheap rooms in the house he had purchased. Ping reasoned he could save rent by bedding down in the cold cellar, and the old man seemed to admire him for that. Lee would give any leftovers from the restaurant to street beggars, whom he met on the way home, whereas Ping would try to sell his scraps. Lee had seen so much suffering that he had developed compassion for the underdog, while Ping just grew indifferent. Lee admitted this attitude seemed to pay off for Ping, until now.

'What good are his fancy cars and houses now,' he thought. 'It looks like he might well lose everything, including his freedom.' Lee felt sad until he realised that he personally, had nothing to lose, for he had nothing in life worth losing.

He also knew what the verdict would be in regard to himself, but not to his friends.

He had done a deal with the prosecutor who bluntly informed him, 'I know you're innocent of the smuggling charge; and you know you're innocent, but if you want the jury to know, you'll have to testify against your buddies … you can walk today, or I'll see you do ten years, sunshine.'

The prosecutor also promised that his other charges could be considered as misdemeanours, if Lee co-operated.

Through despair and panic, Lee agreed to turn Queen's Evidence against Ping, but not La-Lu. He had no regrets about turning on Ping, who had just tried to 'stitch him up' but couldn't bear the idea of hurting La-Lu, whom he realised he now loved more than ever.

But the prosecutor continued, 'This is a package deal, all or nothing. If you agree you'll get off with probation and a fine, and be free to sleep in your own bed tonight.' This suddenly seemed a very attractive option to Lee, who had spent the last six months on remand in Brixton prison. When the prosecutor threw in the carrot of a residential visa, Lee reluctantly accepted the deal.

The jury noted Lee's obvious distress in testifying against La-Lu, even though he tried to be as economical with the truth as he dared. Ping Hey's barrister then interrogated Lee stating no one could be so blindly naïve as to what was really going on, but Lee had to admit he had always been naïve, and trusted no one. This statement was verified by La-Lu who told the court that Ping was the complete opposite of Lee for although they had known each other for many years, Ping always put Ping first.

It now appeared he was prepared to sacrifice anyone for his own ends.

All three were held in the cells, while the jury deliberated. Ping was furious at Lee for testifying against him and was already considering methods of payback. When they were told a verdict had been reached, all three were escorted back to the court, now pregnant with anticipation.

In his summing-up the judge concluded Lee Fong had seen the error of his ways, and was truly repentant. Nevertheless, he was sentenced to eighteen months, which included a year's suspended sentence but with time already served on remand this meant he was now a free man, although he was 'bound over' to keep the peace for two years, and also banned from owning a dog for five years.

Lee Fong was at a loss to fathom how 'not owning a dog' was some form of punishment, for he saw these creatures as noisy, dirty, smelly, flea-ridden vermin, which served only one purpose; to be killed for food.

The judge also considered the prospect of a stiff fine but decided against it for he figured, rightly so, that Lee Fong didn't have 'two pennies to rub together'. The judge had always considered drugs to be a bigger scourge to society than even pornography and was aware that pure heroin is worth more than its weight in gold. So he took great delight in sentencing Ping Hey to seven years for the drug offences, and three for public health and hygiene breaches, plus two years concurrent for animal cruelty with a recommendation that he serve at least ten years.

'Your Honour,' cried Ping's barrister, 'My client can't do ten years.'

'Let him try his best,' the judge wryly responded, recommending deportation when Ping was finally released. It was at this point that everyone in court, including Ping, realised his life was virtually over; by the time he was freed he would be past his prime, with no assets, or contacts. Ping Hey felt his life was now on hold; as if he had just escaped from the orphanage and was starting all over again, for he now realised he had just lost everything.

In a fit of rage, he bit his lip and spat at the judge. He had Hepatitis and was HIV positive; he hoped to anoint the judge with these afflictions, but the judge, who had seen such reactions before, quickly ducked down behind the Bench. Ping was then forced to make a quick exit down the concrete steps, with some able assistance from the guards. La-Lu was sentenced to a mere five years, the jury viewing her as a pawn of the evil Ping, but on hearing the verdict both she and Lee openly wept.

She was then dragged off to await transportation to prison, while Lee heard the judge declare that he was now free to go but advised him not to leave the court immediately, to avoid the swarm of media hovering outside. While he waited, he was told he could say goodbye to his old friends, if he so chose.

He wanted to speak to Ping first, and was shown into a small room with a metal grill behind a partition. After a few minutes he heard ranting from behind the wall as Ping stomped into view. Lee was shocked by his appearance. His face was badly bruised where he had apparently tripped down the steps from the docks, and he was still shaking with rage. He was not a happy man. 'Judas,' he screamed at Lee, 'all your fault - you is gutless swine,' he stormed. 'You let me down, I get you both for this.'

Lee objected, 'You turned on me first,' he declared. 'You tried to fit me up, to take the fall for you.' Ping was in no mood for discussion.

'You wait,' he screamed in Mandarin, 'you die now. You both die; you and bitch La-Lu.' At this juncture Lee left the room; there was no point in staying. As he waited to see La-Lu he sat alone and thought how trusting he had been to both Ping and La-Lu, and how his naïvety had finally caught up with him.

Faith in his friends and moreover, human nature, was now shattered. He could not believe how stupid he'd been, and it was not a good feeling.

He was then shown in to see La-Lu and learned she was going to Holloway, the high security women's prison. He was relieved, in a way. It meant Ping could not reach her there. He saw at once that she had been crying, but she bravely met his gaze until the shock of memory glazed her mind, forcing her to retreat once more, into some hard shell of dark experience. As Lee stared at her he realised she had inherited yet another vision to enhance her tapestry of horrors. She had turned away as scars of pain unfurled to etch their cruel despair in her furtive glance.

Finally, she looked at him, and said, 'Lee, I'm so sorry, involving you in all this; it's all my fault.'

'No,' he objected, 'it's all Ping's fault. He blackmailed you into smuggling the drugs for him.'

'Yes,' she replied, 'but I wanted what he had; the money, the power, the respect. And … I wanted you, Lee,' she confessed.

'All I ever wanted in life was to marry and have a family.' She reached for his hand, but all they could do was place their fingers against either side of the plastic grill. She avoided his eyes, as he confessed he could never father children because of a severe attack of mumps in the orphanage, but only La-Lu could sense the true irony in that statement.

'Let's not dwell on the past,' she said at last. 'The fact is I am guilty, and I have to pay the price, so let's not discuss the case, for we've only got a few minutes.'

She then said, in a subdued voice. 'I wanted to tell you Lee … I have always loved you, and had such plans for us but you were so poor that I wanted to wait until I got some money together, for I was sure you would reject me if you discovered what I was doing.'

Lee sighed with relief. Now he understood; he could neither read nor write, and knew he would be poor for the rest of his life. Up to now he could never understand this thing called love; was it need, or desire, or perhaps power?

He now realised, too late, it was mostly sacrifice; in the purity of being able to give freely with no expectation of return.

He thought to himself that this love must only occur when the other person's happiness becomes more important than your own.

Until now each of them had been mainly concerned with themselves but neither realised, as they sat together, that a dramatic series of events would radically alter their futures.

La-Lu continued, 'Lee, I want you to write to me, in prison, and promise to wait for me; will you do that?' she asked, not realising Lee had never learned to write.

'Of course,' he said uneasily. He had never known a woman's love, and now that he did it was to be at a distance, but he resolved to stay free, work hard and be able to provide for her on her release.

The prison van soon arrived and they had just moments to pledge their devotion, before she had to leave. As their eyes spoke farewell through the plastic grill Lee now became a broken man, as he watched her sitting so alone, crying like a fire in the wind. He began to feel a lump rise in his throat, which he had never felt before, so drank some water from the drinking fountain. It did not help, for he kept trying to swallow and wondered if it was due to the central heating in the courtroom. He went down the steps and was let out by a side door into the street. It was raining, but Lee Fong never noticed.

He arrived back at the house owned by Ping Hey, and squeaked open the front door, trudging up three flights of stairs to his little attic room. On the landing he was confronted by the sight of two black plastic bags outside his door. Must check those in a minute, he thought, but as he was trying the key to his room he heard High Fat, the caretaker, approaching.

'No go in!' he squealed; 'me change lock. You no live here no more.'

Lee persisted with the key, but was getting no-where. 'Got to get in for my stuff,' he insisted.

'All stuff here,' High Fat retorted, pointing to the two bags that contained Lee's clothes, which were his only possessions. 'Why you no in 'plison', where you belong?' He obviously thought Lee Fong was going to be locked up with the others, and had packed his gear.

'You find new place; you no live here no more,' he shouted. 'Take back deposit; find new room,' he said, thrusting some money into Lee's pocket.

'This your money; you keep: no spend - get room - you no live here no more.'

Lee knelt to check the bags and left, grateful that the false passport, which Ping had supplied, was still there as this was his only means of identification. He reflected that soon High Fat would be in a similar predicament when the court repossessed the house. Trudging down the stairs to the street, he smiled with irony, until he realised it was still raining. He was now homeless, in London.

Not a good situation for anyone, especially a poor illiterate Chinaman, he thought. At least it was still light, so he headed to his old place of work, but was shocked to find the little restaurant already boarded up. However, clambering over a side fence to the back yard, where the garbage bins were kept, he found a dry place to spend the night.

I may be out in the open, but at least I'm sheltered from the worst of the weather by the bins, he thought. He did not notice the cold for he was exhausted, and soon fell asleep, content in the knowledge he was now a free man. He resolved that in the morning he would get as far away as he could, having decided big cities often destroy people.

Come morning, Lee awoke to sunshine, and found his clothes had dried out. Having some money in his pocket, he now felt better than he had for ages. He strolled down the road to the nearest 'greasy-spoon' café, where he tucked into a cheap breakfast.

As he ate he considered his situation; 'I will head for Hastings on the coast and find a room there, for I know it's much cheaper than London, which is why Ping bought the bungalow there.'

He liked Hastings, especially the beach and the huge park, where the two of them often kidnapped dogs. He knew the area well. Sifting his belongings into a single bag, keeping only essentials, he disposed of some summer clothes.

He decided to take the tube, from Leicester Square to Charing Cross Station, where he would catch the train to Hastings. He bought a cup of powdered tea from a dispensing machine and ambled over to the ticket office. There were a number of booths and the rush hour had passed, so he got served quickly, and headed for the escalators.

He queued for the long steep escalators and nearly caught his plastic bag in the metal ribs at the bottom.

Lee hated tube-trains, which seemed to epitomise indifference to the masses who had to endure their clamour on a daily basis. As he perched on the platform, awaiting its arrival, he felt a blast of stale air, heralding the thunder of a train.

He had always suffered from a nagging claustrophobia, which would, on occasion, catch him unawares. He had fought these panic attacks, as he called them, all his life. He never felt at ease in crowded places and tube trains brought out the worst in him. He suddenly realised, with a surreal sense of panic that his future now seemed bleak and purposeless, but that he could free himself in an instant, by jumping in front of the oncoming train. He knew it was a method used by some people to erase the agony of mental anguish. He had experienced enough of that to realise it far exceeded physical pain, to which one could sometimes adapt and even accept.

As these thoughts rushed through his mind like the wind in the tunnel he found himself gripping a pillar, not for physical dependency, but rather the security that holding onto something solid would slow this sudden impulse he now felt to simply hurl himself a few feet forward into instant oblivion. He knew just one moment of blind pain would totally eradicate all his problems. He realised that timing would be critical, for he had no wish to end up like a vegetable for the rest of his life, if he did happen to survive the impact.

He stared transfixed as the beast thundered towards him, but suddenly a vision of the lovely La-Lu flashed across his mind, and he shut his eyes tightly. Some instinct within him sensed that if he could not see the train approaching, he would be unable to gauge his 'exit', even though he had relaxed his grip on the pillar.

In a split second he heard the first carriage thunder past as the train ground to a noisy halt.

A small spark of his love for La-Lu had ignited some deep desire to live, so he proceeded to squeeze into the crowded carriage, where he found all the seats occupied. He was now surrounded by total strangers, who stared briefly, but blankly into his face. It was a short journey to the main-line station of Charing Cross.

The rush hour was ending so the queue for the ticket booths at the main station was short. He asked for a ticket to Warrior Square, Hastings. The attendant queried, 'Single,' and informed him that an express would be leaving on platform twelve in ten minutes, so he purchased a one-way ticket, and found he had time for a coffee from the vending machine. As he shouldered his bag and ran for the train, he tossed his plastic cup into a nearby bin, just missing a stump-toed pigeon limping past.

He watched as a passing skinhead suddenly stomped on the bird with his huge boots, crushing it instantly, and Lee reflected with some surprise, how little compassion he had felt for this poor creature's demise.

He rushed for the train, but once aboard felt relaxed. This is a fresh start for sure, he thought, wondering what sort of job he would find in Hastings. He loved train journeys, except on the Tube. He had once fallen down a long escalator, and as he lay stunned at the bottom, everybody had just walked over him.

He was so glad to escape London, the restaurant, and Ping Hey. Again he thought of La-Lu, and his mood changed to sadness. He was at a loss what to do.

I must get a decent job, he thought; a proper job, and save up for a nice home. In five years she will be free; if we got married she could stay with me, as my wife. And … we could have a lovely home, living together.

The Virgin Express 'Pendolino' was quiet and smooth, being one of the latest tilting trains, which angled over when rounding a bend. Lee relaxed and reflected on his past; like the times in the orphanage with Ping and La-Lu, but recalled some happy memories like the holiday outing on the anniversary of Chairman Mao's birthday. Only the boys were allowed to go on the trip, but of course the girls wanted all the news when they returned. He smiled as he remembered trying to explain to La-Lu what his visit to the seaside was like, for she had never seen the sea.

She cornered him as soon as he got back and begged to be told all about the waves. She was so young and innocent then, and so different.

Lee felt happy as he tilted his seat back and daydreamed about the happiest day of his life. He recalled how he tried to explain his vision of the sea to La-Lu. He thought back to their conversation.

'Have you really seen the sea?' she cried. 'What's it like? Tell me all about it?'

'We had to travel in a smelly old bus for hours, over the hills and mountains,' he told her.

'Go on?' she pleaded.

'Well, it all starts as you drive down from the mountains to where the land levels out, and then you can see it in the distance, stretching for a hundred miles, glinting and sparkling in the sun.' She looked aghast.

He continued. 'The clouds and mist just disappear and the wind dies down. Then you see the waves, shining in the sun and moving all the time, back and forth.'

'Oh, what are they like, please describe them for me?'

'Well, all you see is a straight line of water in front of of you, called the horizon, and everything out there is the ocean which flows up to, and over the beach,' he told her.

'What's the beach?' she interrupted.

'It's made from sand; fine white sand, miles and miles of it,' he replied. 'The water swishes and surges, and makes foam that rolls onto the beach,' he continued.

'Why doesn't the beach sink?' she queried.

'Because it soaks the water up, until it drains back into the sea,' he replied.

'Ping and I tried to dig down to the bottom of the sand, but it goes on for ever,' he told her.

'To the other side of the Earth?' she puzzled.

'Don't know,' he replied. 'Maybe.'

'So what happens to all the foam,' she inquired, 'is that the wave?'

'It's part of the wave … the waves make foam all the time, called surf, and it forms when they come crashing down on each other,' he explained.

'How many waves are there, where do they come from?'

'There are usually three, in a row, and they start far out on the ocean,' he replied.

'And did you see all three of them?' she asked.

'It's not like that … they come, and they go. They disappear, but new ones take their place,' he explained.

'What do you mean?' she said, confused.

'Well, they start far out at sea, and steadily grow bigger, but then they swell up and collapse down on themselves, turning into surf. This is when they 'break', as it's called, before new waves start to form.'

'How big are they?' she asked.

'Sometimes ten or even twelve feet high, and that's why people drown,' he told her.

'Wow,' she exclaimed, 'but why is the sand not washed away when these big waves break onto the beach?'

'It's difficult to explain,' he answered. 'Only the little ones end up on the beach; they are only inches high but the big ones break far out at sea.'

'So when you go for a swim, you start with the little waves?' she asked.

'Yes, for the waves themselves are very long. The beach sweeps gently down, to join the sea, but stretches sideways for miles.'

He wanted to tell her about the little beach crabs, which scuttled back and forth chasing the foaming tide, but decided against it remembering his failed attempts on the trip to explain the colour of the wind to a blind boy, who had asked him that question.

He continued. 'It can be very dangerous; people drown by swallowing the waves ... when they cannot get away.'

'I thought waves were beautiful,' she cried. 'Why don't they close their mouth and walk back to the beach?'

'Because the waves will drag you under the water, and can sweep you off your feet and carry you far out to sea, where you drown and then your body gets washed back onto the beach.'

She paused to reflect, and he wondered at her innocence. He felt sad that she had not been able to visit the sea.

He tried to explain to her, 'Once you get past the big waves, the sea becomes calm and level, right up to the horizon.' He wanted to convey the atmosphere to La-Lu. 'The waves can move quickly, or slowly, depending on the wind and the tides.'

'Tides!' she exclaimed.

'Like currents, in a river.' La-Lu had once paddled in a river; it was actually a sewer, but she didn't know that. 'The moon affects the size of the waves, like it affects people. Did you know some people go crazy on a full moon, and of course it affects women, some of the time?'

She didn't, but answered, 'Yes.'

He continued. 'When the moon grows big the seas also grow, and that's usually when people drown. Sometimes when you see a big wave coming you can turn your back to it, so that it washes right over you, but the wave after that one might be even bigger and could catch you by surprise. If you're off balance you will be pushed over and sucked under the water. It's called - *going out of your depth.'*

'Why not hold your breath, until it gets calm again?' she queried.

'It's not as simple as that, for you get confused, tumbling under the water. You don't even know which way is up to the surface. Besides you are choking, and the sand and the salt sting your eyes, and blind you.' He paused for these implications to register.

'So you swallow a lot of water and drown!' she concluded.

'No, what happens is you get some water in your lungs, but that makes your throat close up, to stop you sucking in any more. It's an automatic reflex, but you can't breathe so your brain gets starved of air, and goes to sleep.'

'And you drown!' La-Lu surmised.

'Usually, but sometimes people who have been under the water for half-an-hour are washed up on the beach and are given help to breathe again. But, if they do recover, they usually have damage to their brain and cannot talk or walk normally any more,' Lee explained.

'So why do people go in the sea, if it can kill them?' she asked.

'Because they love the feeling of the water all around them; they can turn in any direction and feel the waves cool them down in the hot sun. I love it,' Lee concluded.

'Love it !' cried La-Lu, in surprise.

'Yes, ... just before the waves break they seem to balance for a moment, as the wind whips a long crest of spray along the top, and as they collapse you can see this misty spray floating in the air, like a little rainbow; there is so much beauty and power in a big wave,' he told her.

'Is it a challenge for you, then?' she asked.

'In a way,' he answered, 'because it is very refreshing, as well as dangerous and noisy.'

'Noisy! ... As well?' she responded.

'Yes, I should have told you. Waves are always noisy.'

'What, even at night?' she queried.

'Yes,' he answered. 'All the time, day and night; especially at night, when you hear them a long way off, crashing down on each other.'

La-Lu was very quiet then, like she was when the judge passed sentence on her in Court that morning.

Lee was jarred out of his daydream by the sound of the ticket-collector.

'Tickets, please, all tickets, please?

Next stop Hastings .... Hastings, next stop.'

The train soon arrived at the station and deposited Lee at Warrior Square Station. It was time for a new start.

CHAPTER THREE

Lee Fong arrived in Hastings just after midday. It was cloudy and windy, and he was tired and hungry.

He knew exactly where his old friend Ping had hidden a set of spare keys to the bungalow, in nearby St. Leonards. It took him less than twenty minutes to walk there, through Alexander Park, where he stopped for a cheap snack at the park café. He noticed that all the tables and chairs were new, and the veranda there had acquired a large canopy, which the new owners told him was to shelter the dog-walkers who patronised the premises. Lee was not fond of dogs, but appreciated the canopy, as the threat of rain lay dormant in dark clouds overhead.

He reached the bungalow around two in the afternoon, but was surprised to find it completely boarded up. He retrieved the keys where Ping had hidden them, months before. He got confused when he tried to open the front door in vain, but suddenly realised the locks must have been changed. He then spotted a notice proclaiming the fact that the property had been re-possessed and was now in the hands of the Official Receivers, and subject to Court proceedings.

'That didn't take long,' thought Lee, with growing apprehension, for now he had nowhere to stay, and no bed for the night. He decided not to break in and risk losing his freedom again so threw the keys into the bushes and headed back down to the park café, to reflect on his current dilemma, over a lingering cup of coffee.

He considered he should still have enough money to rent a cheap room, so headed into town to Queens Road, which hosted all the local estate agents, but after a few brief enquiries Lee quickly realised what he was up against. Apparently he needed not just a month's rent in advance, but a similar amount as a 'returnable' deposit, plus a couple of hundred pounds in processing fees.

Not only that, but he would need an employer's reference and three months' current bank statements together with photographic ID, which he did possess, in the form of the Chinese passport that Ping had procured for him. Lee now realised he could only afford to pay for a room on a weekly basis, so he headed for the St. Leonards' area of Hastings, which he knew was a lot cheaper, but a lot rougher. He knew that dozens of different nationalities inhabited this area, but decided he might actually feel more at home in that vicinity. He scoured the area for a cheap room but could only find a 'Bed and Breakfast' establishment, which was prepared to consider a cheaper tariff for weekly stays.

This, he realised, would deplete most of his funds after only a week, but would give him the chance to find a job and a more permanent abode.

He found he would have just twenty pounds left to last the week, for 'essentials' like food and cigarettes, so he resolved to quit smoking immediately. Anyway, this had been his ambition for years and now seemed an opportune time.

His tiny room seemed clean enough, and even housed a small television, which he spent most of the time watching.

The first night he was awoken by an itching sensation on his face. As he blinked open one eye he saw a little insect, brown in colour, perched right on the end of his nose. The creature seemed to throb as its skin pulsated to a redder hue. He had seen these things before, and realised immediately it was a bed-bug. He suddenly recalled Ping telling him about the time he went to Lanzarote and visited a 'bug-farm', where cochineal bugs were bred on cactus plants. When matured, the bugs were sun-dried and crushed to produce carminic acid, which is widely used in food products, by firms like Starbucks. In addition to food, this dried bug-blood is also used in cosmetic products like lipsticks, and pill-coatings.

As they stared at each other Lee slowly realised that this bug, on the end of his nose, was steadily drinking blood; fresh blood: *his* blood. He soon became wide awake and quickly brushed the creature off his nose. Then he squeezed it onto the bed, where it left a bright red smear on the clean white sheet.

Climbing out of the bed, he noticed on the ceiling above him, a line of the creatures trekking their way from a corner of the room, over to where he slept.

He knew the heat from the bed was attracting them, so reached for his cigarette lighter. As they parachuted down from the ceiling above he was able to spot them land and torch them in an instant.

They would immediately swell up and explode with a slight pop. Despite his frustration at having a sleepless night, he took gratuitous delight in disposing of them all, until the trail dried up.

In the morning he confronted the landlady who became very obnoxious, declaring that in thirty years none of her faithful tenants had ever raised such monstrous accusations and that he would have to vacate the premises at the end of the week, which he planned to do at any rate.

However, he partook of her meagre continental breakfast, consisting of croissant, orange juice, toast and tea, which he felt should tide him over for a few hours.

He determined to look for work as a kitchen porter, and to visit the housing authority, where he hoped his luck would change. He had shaved and donned a white shirt, his only one, which he graced with a flashy tie and neat jacket. The tie was a 'Christmas Special' given to him by Ping and had a prominent button, which played a Christmas tune when pressed. Fortunately, the battery had long expired, for he couldn't imagine the reaction at an interview if it went off accidentally.

He walked from his digs in Warrior Square up London Road where he found the local Housing Office, situated in the basement of a church annex, which had been sold to the council when the church needed funds.

After a long wait, he was ushered into a room where his 'Statement of Circumstances' was taken. He was told that although he had lived and worked in England for years it was unlikely he would be allocated anywhere for some time as there were thousands before him in the queue.

If he had admitted to an addiction, or claimed asylum as a refugee, his points total would have been much higher but it was too late for all that.

He was advised to find some sort of job and sofa-surf with friends, until he had enough reserves to rent a place as the council could not help him, at the moment, because he was not even homeless. He was allocated a placing in Band D, but was advised, if he could produce medical history of some disablement or addiction, he would escalate up the ladder. He was also advised that if he did end up on the streets, to adopt a dog, as a weekly allowance was paid for this, on top of his benefits.

So Lee, who hated dogs, but had a roof over his head, which he shared with an army of parasitic bed-bugs, was now at a loss what to do. He was advised to register with a local doctor, and a dentist, but even this proved impossible for he had neither a Medical Card nor a National Insurance Number. Eventually he managed to register at the Employment Exchange for work, by producing his fake passport, but they had no record of his employment history. Although he was prepared to take any work available, he had no transport, which limited his options, and apparently it would be weeks before his claim could be processed. He couldn't say he had worked for Ping as that would really complicate matters.

He then scoured all the hotels and restaurants in the area looking for casual work but even the kitchen-porter jobs were all taken, due to a high influx of immigrants, prepared to work for half the wages of the indigenous workforce.

He needed another shirt, so went to the nearest 'thrift-shop', where he found a decent specimen on sale for a couple of pounds. On leaving the shop he spotted somebody stuffing clothes down their trousers, and informed the assistant. She told him, 'We have to tolerate this abuse for most of those rascals carry knives and we're only volunteers, so we're not even insured. They wear those clothes until they're dirty, then give them back to us, as a donation, and steal a new outfit. Sometimes they even take something they've had before, but now it's been cleaned and ironed, they've had their washing done for nothing.'

By frequenting the various soup kitchens around town, and receiving food parcels from the food-banks, Lee was able to survive after leaving his 'Bed and Breakfast'. The Salvation Army had given him a good sleeping bag, and he soon found a spot in the local park beside the Bowling-Club shelter, where he could tuck up in the bag until it became light; then arise to hide it behind bushes.

He went to Heron House, in London Road, where he learned that if he could find a landlord prepared to wait six weeks until his housing claim came through they would pay all the rent provided he could raise the security deposit.

Eventually, a passing patrol car found him sleeping in the park and told him to clear off or he would be arrested, so he headed for the seafront where he had spotted various people sleeping on the beach and even on benches.

He spoke to a few down-and-outs who warned him to avoid the benches, as teenage thugs would come out of the clubs late at night and pick on homeless people in sleeping bags. If their victim were asleep they would urinate over them; then beat and kick them, for the victim's arms and legs would be inside the bag, leaving them helpless.

Most of the people sleeping rough were, like himself, new in town. They all seemed to have substance abuse problems and many were even prescribed Methadone, by the National Health Service, to wean them off their heroin addiction.

Mostly, they were just simple alcoholics with a hard-luck story, which often explained their predicament. Most of the area was designated an alcohol-free-zone, so they had little choice but to frequent the local park, where they could conceal their can of beer in a paper bag. The more hardened who took to spirits, would buy a soft drink, pour most of it away and top up with cheap Vodka, or whatever.

It was on one of his ventures to the park that Lee fell in with a group of veteran junkies. As was the custom most possessed fearsome dogs, which helped protect them when they slept rough. It so happened that as Lee sat down one of these dogs urinated on his only pair of trousers. He had already stepped in some dog mess, and couldn't seem to get rid of the smell, so he lashed out at the dog, but the owner came over and head-butted him. A scuffle ensued, and some passers-by called the police. Lee and his assailant were charged with disorderly conduct and being drunk in public. They were taken to the cells and appeared before local magistrates the following morning, when they were both given Anti-Social-Behaviour-Orders and 'bound over' to keep the peace.

Lee had made peace with his opponent, who relished his ASBO, seen as another badge of honour by the street people.

Lee had now been in town for over a month, and had acquired many friends; even witnessing some of them die in the squalid squats they inhabited. When one of these poor wretches managed to secure a room or a flat they would happily invite their cronies back, to sofa-surf. Unfortunately, in such dismal conditions drugs and drink ruled their world.

Drink was the most abused, but everyone seemed to take 'weed' or cannabis. After a spell of this, when the novelty wore off they would end up 'chasing the dragon', which is slang for smoking heroin.

Over-indulgence in drugs, or sex, follows the law of diminishing returns, so most ended up 'jacking' or main-lining heroin straight into their veins.

On one visit to a soup kitchen Lee went to the Gents toilet to find a guy slumped dead, with a syringe stuck in his neck.

He knew from dealing with junkies in London that this method was only used as a last resort. Initially it was arms and legs but as the veins shrunk an injection straight into the groin would give an instant hit; but real die-hards had to resort to jacking between their toes, and eventually the jugular vein in their neck, as the only access.

Even when they were on daily doses of Methadone, some would sell or swop their bottle for a bit of heroin, or even a rock of crack-cocaine.

Eventually the authorities caught on, and 'customers' had to consume the liquid in the chemists, right in front of the pharmacist.

Lee soon discovered there were hundreds of derelict properties in St. Leonards, and found a squat in a huge abandoned building, which he shared with a few others. They ripped up the floorboards to use as firewood, but this caused the actual house to catch fire, and the resultant furore meant everyone was chucked out because although the owner could not be traced the media got involved and the Council lost no time in boarding the place up.

Lee's staple diet was now a dirt-cheap cider as that particular brand had never smelled an apple, being concocted mostly from chemicals.

One of the friends he shared the squat with had just died so Lee and the others decided to go to the crematorium to pay their last respects.

This guy was an ardent follower of Pink Floyd and his favourite song was 'Dark Side Of The Moon'. On the line-up of wreaths at the funeral were five single ones, with the letters, D-S-O-T-M, on each.

It was not until he met up with the family at the 'wake', in a local pub, that he learned the significance of the five wreaths. After his first decent meal for ages he left the reception for 'Bottle Alley' on Hastings seafront, where a group of the homeless stood with Lee in a circle and together, as one, poured their beers on the ground in silent tribute to their deceased comrade.

One of the groups had broken through the door of a boarded-up basement flat, so five of them decided to squat there. It was completely empty but did have a toilet and sink. They managed to turn the water on but realised there was no electric feed to the premises so some bright 'spark' pushed a couple of nails through the meter wires, and behold ... there was light. One day when they were out shoplifting for food the place was burgled. All their possessions and clothes had gone and the flat was totally trashed.

They decided they would not be pushed out, so they purchased a sturdy lock for the door.

One of them got arrested while shoplifting, so now only four remained. There was Lee, an old man called Turk, and a young couple. It would soon be summer, but it was still very cold and the absence of heating greatly affected them. It was difficult to wash in cold water and keeping clothes clean was a nightmare.

One night, Lee got a bad attack of asthma so, to keep him warm, it was decided the young girl should cuddle up to him that night.

He was half asleep when he felt her wrap her arms around him. Earlier that day he had collected his pittance of benefit from the Post Office. This was barely enough to live on, but now that he had an address of sorts, he was entitled to something. When he awoke he needed a drink so searched his pockets for change, but all his money had been taken; the girl and her friends had disappeared, leaving him all alone. He was once again isolated, penniless and friendless with neither food nor clothes.

He wandered outside and asked the advice of some street people in Bottle Alley.

He was advised to apply for a flat in one of the new tower blocks, where one of their friends had recently been housed. He went to the Housing Trust, where he was told he would need to be officially homeless to be allocated a place there and because he already had a roof over his head, this was not the case. He informed them that he no longer felt safe there and needed to move, but was then told that if he moved out under his own free will he would be deemed as making himself voluntarily homeless, so they would never rehouse him.

He was also told that if he slept inside a rubbish dumpster, covered by a tarpaulin, he would not be classified as homeless; only if there were no coverings on the dumpster, could he be classed as having no abode. However, his dilemma was solved on returning to the squat. There were fire engines and police cars gathered outside, as billowing clouds of smoke cascaded into the street. Apparently, someone had set the place on fire, and it was now totally gutted.

So Lee went back again to the Housing Trust, who were able to confirm that his home had indeed been torched, and providentially he could not have done it, as he had been present in the housing office at the time. Because of that, he was now officially homeless, and had enough points to be placed into 'Band-A', ... which now qualified him for the immediate allocation of his own private premises.

He gratefully accepted a flat in one of the tower blocks, but was told he could not move in until the following day. He had no money or food, so set off for the Salvation Army where Captain Steve listened to his plight, fed him, and furnished him with a sleeping bag. He did not relish bumping into any of his old friends as he feared a confrontation over his missing money.

He learned from the other street people that the young couple with whom he shared the flat had made a big 'score' of heroin that very day, so it seemed that they had come into some easy money. He was also pretty sure it was they who had torched the place, as nobody else had keys.

He decided against spending the night in one of his usual haunts, and laid his sleeping bag beneath the huge tunnel, connecting the two underground car parks. This seemed a wise decision for heavy rain was forecast that evening. He settled down in the early hours but was rudely awoken by a torrent of water cascading down the tunnel. Before he could extricate himself from the bag he was washed down the tunnel, ending up in a nearby exit. After recovering from this flash-flood he found himself stranded with a ruined sleeping bag, no possessions and no money; he was also tired and hungry and depressed. However next day, after collecting the keys, he was able to move straight into a renovated flat in Roosevelt Towers. This, he hoped, was a fresh start and a chance to get his life back on track.

CHAPTER FOUR

Lee found it a struggle to survive on less than sixty pounds a week, now that he had bills to pay in regards to his new abode. He was not used to forking out for electric and gas and water, and having got his appetite back, now discovered he couldn't afford to eat properly.

He went to the drop-in medical centre adjacent to Hastings railway station, where he could be seen without the formality of a medical card. He confessed he now had a severe drink problem, and a kindly doctor registered him as 'alcoholic'. This meant he could claim Disability Living Allowance, or DLA, meaning a substantial boost to his funds, whereby he might even be able to save a few pounds a week, for emergencies.

As the weeks passed, La-Lu was never far from his mind and he resolved to visit her in prison when he could afford the fare. She was a long way off, in Holloway, and this meant a long journey there and back so he would have little time to spend with her when he did arrive.

He could not afford to stay overnight in London so decided the best option would be to drive there and back. He knew he would have to apply for a visiting order, but realised this would draw attention to his presence and he could be placed on a watch-list.

Lee had been taught the rudiments of driving by Ping, who sometimes let him drive on their travels to Hastings; but he had only acquired the basic fundamentals and his knowledge of the Highway Code was sadly lacking. However, in a month or so, he had managed to save enough money to purchase an old car from one of his cronies. He guessed it was probably pinched, being such a bargain, at two hundred pounds. He considered that because he didn't have a licence anyway, it didn't really matter if it was, or not.

He knew he couldn't insure it, but as the car did have a couple of months on the Tax disc before it expired, he felt it would be safe to take on an early morning drive to London; then a quiet cruise back in the middle of the night. He knew that on the motorway, with little traffic about, there was very little chance of being stopped by the police.

He set off very early the next morning to avoid the rush hour but after a few hours on the motorway stopped for a cup of coffee and a sandwich at a service station. He was stunned when the bill came to nearly ten pounds, and upset for he had hoped to buy La-Lu a small present, but now his funds were almost depleted for he was left with just two five-pound notes, and a few pennies.

When he arrived at the prison he had to sign the visitors' book, and realised by giving his name and address he was well and truly 'on the radar'. After a long wait, with other visitors in a bleak room, he was ushered into a large hall.

La-Lu was perched at a metal table and he scarcely recognised her; she was drawn and haggard and instinctively he knew why she looked so emaciated. She was on drugs! She gave him an embarrassed hug, and he responded with a quick kiss. She noticed immediately that Lee was shocked by her appearance.

As he sat down and took her hands, he noticed long scars on her wrists. He knew what this meant, but as he looked at her arm, he also saw track marks, which meant she was now injecting heroin. The look of despair in his eyes was too much to bear, and she broke down, weeping uncontrollably.

They had not spoken as yet, but she sobbed, 'I'm so sorry, Lee. I had no choice. It's a living hell in here for someone like me.'

He queried how she had gotten heroin inside the prison, but she explained anything was available for a price. Accomplices outside the walls would fill a tennis ball with heroin and throw it over the high walls, in the middle of the night. Next day the daily gardener would collect and deliver it, and woe-betide anyone else who retrieved it, for the whole prison knew to whom it belonged and everyone else would have to ignore it, if they happened to stumble across it.

The prison had been put in lockdown the previous day, when one of the inmates hanged herself in her cell, so an aura of suspicion and fear permeated the whole prison. Lee felt the hopeless abandonment, which seemed almost palpable.

He was still happy to spend an hour or so with La-Lu, for they needed a heart-to-heart talk. They did not bring up the past except to relate news that had filtered through, about Ping's lawyer working on his appeal, where he might even be granted early parole. La-Lu had no financial reserves, so had resigned herself to many more years of confinement.

Although La-Lu could write letters from the prison, Lee could not read very well, so they resolved to keep in contact by phone.

He apologised for neglecting her, and explained what a hard time he had gone through, promising to be more faithful now that he was settled. La-Lu was not permitted to ring out, but Lee could still ring her inside the prison. He had purchased a cheap phone for ten pounds, so promised to stay in touch as they continued to chat about her demise into this dark world.

He still had the five-pound notes, which he wanted to give her, but she was unable to accept these over the counter. He slid them under the table, where she had to slip them up under her dress, to a place the authorities would be reluctant to look when the women were searched on their return to the cells.

As this surreptitious movement was being enacted Lee could see an officer, at the desk overlooking the visitors, glaring at him and he started to sweat; however, La-Lu kept calm. He now worried that he might be apprehended as he left the prison and possibly end up in a different one. Apparently all the inmates got searched after a visit to avoid contraband like drugs or money entering the system, although half the prison personnel would enhance their wages by smuggling in everything from porn videos to mobile phones.

La-Lu and Lee then made a solemn promise to help each other. She swore she would get help with her addiction, and he promised to find a job and prepare a home for them, ready for her release. She pledged her love and he promised to be faithful, as they bid each other a fond farewell. He was apprehensive on leaving the confines of the prison but nobody stopped him on the way out, so once he had settled in his car he relaxed and set off for the long drive home.

He now had time to reflect on his visit and the pledges they had made to each other. Although he was again enamoured with the romantic aspect of the love they shared, he was not blind to the reality of the situation.

La-Lu had admitted her addiction, which up to now she had held in denial, telling Lee she could quit anytime, claiming she was in complete control. He knew from experience that all addicts go through that stage, and swear they can handle it, but they usually can't so it ends up destroying many lives, which is why a lot of countries still execute drug smugglers.

The old car was running well, but what Lee didn't realise, although he had checked all the lights and indicators before setting off, was that when braking, only one rear light was working as the bulb had blown on the adjacent side, so it was inevitable that on the long journey home he was pulled over by the local constabulary.

When it was discovered that the car had been reported stolen some months back, and there was no valid insurance or certificate of road-worthiness he was promptly handcuffed and taken to the nearby police station. He underwent a series of methodical procedures. Firstly, his fingerprints and DNA were taken, and next he was ushered into a room where he was totally engulfed by a kind of ultra-violet light. He was told that this light was of a certain spectrum to show up 'black-water', which is a DNA compound used to spray people involved in robberies, when cash is taken. It is indelible and invisible to the human eye, and cannot be washed off the skin or clothes. Lee knew this procedure has a one hundred per cent conviction rate; but he was cleared, although his shoelaces and trouser belt were removed, in case he attempted suicide.

He was led into a twelve-foot square cell where he had the pleasure of a hard mattress just a few inches thick. Luckily the heating system was deployed directly under the bed so at least he was warm. The metal toilet was a challenge for it took him ages to figure out how to flush it. The cell seemed claustrophobic for the top of the walls curved round to meet the ceiling giving it no definition, or sense of boundary, while harsh fluorescent lights constantly saturated the pervasive magnolia décor. He was offered a meal, which arrived on a very hot plastic tray, and appeared to be a microwave special, being practically inedible and totally tasteless.

Lee's car was confiscated and he appeared in the Magistrates Court the following morning to be given six months' custodial sentence, suspended for a year.

The police, who had requisitioned his phone, now returned it so he was able to phone a friend. He rang Tom, a social worker whom Lee had recently been allocated because of his alcoholism. He related well to Tom, who himself had been an alcoholic, but one who still succumbed to temptation on the odd occasion. Tom was assured that his petrol costs would be covered, if he drove up to collect Lee at Hayward's Heath police station.

When Tom turned up he seemed different, but Lee concluded it was the long journey and the hassle of playing Good Samaritan, that was making him so taciturn. After a long silence, Tom spoke out, informing Lee that he had completely given up alcohol, as he had now found religion. Lee didn't know what religion was, but he could see that Tom had changed dramatically. On the long drive home Tom explained that he had been visiting a soup kitchen in his role as a counsellor, when an old lady asked if she could pray for his drink problem. Tom was too embarrassed to refuse and sat alone with her as she held his hand and asked if he was capable of forgiving others. She then asked him if he knew the Lord's Prayer, and when Tom assured her he did, she asked him to recite it. When he reached the verse about ... 'forgiving our trespasses as we forgive others', she asked him if he realised what that actually meant.

He confessed he had never considered the implications, so she explained that when you say that verse you are asking God to forgive you your sins, in the way that you must now forgive others who have sinned against you. 'And,' she continued, 'if you still harbour resentment to others, and don't really forgive them, you are then asking God to treat you with this same resentment, and not to forgive you.'

Tom realised all this seemed logical, and resolved there and then to forgive everybody for past grievances. He knew there was a lot that he needed God to forgive him for, and he didn't want to hedge his bets so decided in that one moment, to forgive everybody everything. The trouble was, the old lady explained, that he also needed to forgive himself as well, if he was to receive the Grace of God.

Tom found this almost impossible, riddled as he was with the guilt that most people shoulder throughout their lives; but the old lady prayed fervently for him and when he resigned himself completely, it seems the spirit of God touched him in some miraculous way. That very evening in the shabby soup kitchen, he was totally freed from his constant desire to have a drink.

They finally reached Hastings and Lee was invited to have lunch with Tom and his partner, who lived in a little cottage in the countryside near Hastings. He was very tired and hungry so he jumped at the chance.

Tom avoided witnessing any more to Lee, but he did persuade him to come to the church that ran the soup kitchen, on the promise of a good meal. Apparently the service would be followed by a short walk, and later a barbecue, weather permitting.

Lee was as good as his word, and met Tom at nine-o-clock that Sunday morning. In the huge Anglican church hundreds of ancient pews channelled the stone-slabbed aisles, leading to an elaborate elevated altar, crowned with a magnificent golden crucifix, itself hallowed by a host of ornate statues glowing softly behind clusters of red candles. The congregation sat in subdued silence as the priest recited a call for people to come to God and repent, but Lee had no hesitation in declining the offer. He had never believed in God, and didn't intend to start now. How could he; he did not even believe in himself. He could not relate to any God who permitted total chaos and lifelong agony for his creations. However, he admired these people for their sincerity, for it was obvious they also suffered the 'slings and arrows of outrageous fortune', as much as unbelievers did.

After the service, Lee and Tom headed for the nearby wood, with about a dozen of the congregation. They gathered in a little valley, where a collection of log-benches surrounded an improvised barbeque. This was just an old oil-drum cut length-wise and fitted with hinges, so the top half served as a lid.

Lee was surprised that it worked so efficiently, but was even more surprised by some of the group, who claimed they were vegetarians, bringing along some Quorn burgers and Soya sausages. He couldn't understand anyone not liking meat, and was amazed such people would even bother attending a barbecue.

However, Tom introduced Lee to a chap who turned out to be the head gardener in the local park. He seemed concerned by Lee's plight and told him he could fix him up with some work at the park, if he didn't mind working outdoors. Lee jumped at this chance and agreed to present himself the following morning to the gardeners' office, beside the huge greenhouse in the park.

Early morning found Lee waiting outside the yard, which housed all the garden machinery. Inside was a little shack, which served as office, mess hall and shelter. He was formally introduced to the others after he agreed to start work as a general clean-up man. This entailed cleaning the five toilets in the park, and picking up litter, not to mention all the dog-mess. He was then told his official job title would be 'refuse disposal officer' and of course, he would start on the minimum wage.

Because Lee had recently had his welfare money suspended for the customary six weeks, as he had missed a medical appointment, he was elated that he could now forego the hassle of claiming welfare, which up to now he still had to do. He had been just a few minutes late for that interview, as he didn't know the area, and it had taken him ages to find the place.

All his DLA had been stopped and he was now back living on a pittance. He had just enough money to eat and pay his water, gas and electric, but that dilemma had the hidden bonus of curtailing his drink problem. He now realised that if he had gone for another medical he would have been signed-off as fit for work, because no alcohol would have been found in his system.

He soon settled into the routine of hosing down the toilets and meandering about with a spidery utensil and shoulder bag to collect the litter, but he found the task of lifting dog mess an ordeal. Some people would put the mess in a little bag and hang it on a nearby branch. To Lee this seemed futile, as he felt it would be better just left on the ground, for the rain to wash away; but in a plastic bag it could hang in the trees for months, if not years. Lee now despised dogs and their vile habits.

He was permitted to drop into the park café for cups of tea to keep warm, and even buy food there at a subsidised price. He was very grateful for this, for until he collected his first wage packet, it was the only way he was able to eat and keep healthy. He soon got to recognise the various regulars who always appeared around the time he ate his breakfast. They were mostly dog-walkers, and they all seemed to know each other and all the different dogs. Lee tried to ignore the dogs but he did speak to the customers, who got to know his name and who appeared to be a very friendly bunch.

However, as summer arrived, Lee was elevated to the status of gardening assistant. He was told that if he persevered in his excellent timekeeping and diligence it would not be long before he would be an official groundsman, with a resultant rise in grade and better wages, above his minimum wage by at least twenty pence per hour.

It so happened that one particular person always sat at the same table as Lee. He was a grizzled old man who apparently had lost his own dog recently. It had been his only companion, as his wife had passed many years previously. Lee had no trouble relating to this 'dog-less' individual, but what surprised him was the fact that all the dogs had now got to recognise him at the café. Even when he was working in the flower beds, pulling weeds or edging the borders, the dogs would bark out a greeting as they ran up to say hello.

Lee was unsure whether to be flattered or annoyed at this intrusion into his life, but he now realised that animals showed him more affection than most of the people he encountered on his travels.

The one exception was the old man. Somehow Lee found he was able to confide in him, and he in turn, saw Lee as a naïve young man who needed guidance. They would sit on the café bench every day and exchange viewpoints, and slowly Lee became educated in the ways of the world.

The old man once asked Lee to close his eyes and tell him what he could hear.

'I can hear the traffic in the distance,' began Lee, 'and the tractor that is cutting the grass.'

'And what else?'

'The dogs barking.'

'Do you hear the distant train?' asked the old man.

'Just about, and the plane flying overhead.'

'But is that all, what about the birds?'

'Of course; the birds, but they are always noisy,' Lee responded.

'Yes, you hear them, but you never listen to them, do you?' he asked.

Lee had to admit that, and the old man explained that many species of birds would sing, not simply because they could, but because they realised they were alive and wanted to prove it. It was, he explained, their way of acknowledging a life force, or an entity greater than themselves.

'You might even say they were paying homage, for the Bible claims all creatures exalt their Creator,' continued the old man.

Lee was surprised at this; here was another person who had little reason to have faith in anything; yet obviously still believed all life had an instinct for this God, whose existence made little sense to him, personally.

When they finished chatting Lee got back to work and was surprised to find that he was actually listening to the birdsong all around him. He was shocked that even when working in the middle of that cacophony he had failed to actually listen, but simply heard it as a mundane background noise, to be buried and ignored in the more serious business of life. Now he realised it was, in fact, part of life itself.

On another occasion, at the café, the old man asked him to listen to the sound of the schoolchildren in the nearby playground during lunch-hour. They could just see them from the café, as they ran around and cavorted, with the boundless energy of youth in total disregard to the chilly winds sweeping the area.

'In the old days I used to come here with my little dog and walk past the school fence. The kids would come running over to pet the dog, and I would hand them biscuits to feed him, but those days are long gone.

Now you dare not speak to a child, never mind give them biscuits.'

Lee agreed that times had changed, and not for the better. He asked the old man if he felt all this political correctness was totally necessary.

'Oh, absolutely, my friend,' he replied. 'Not just because of paedophilia and the like, but mainly because of the insidious workings of the internet, which all kids have access to these days, because of their mobile phones.

There are over a thousand kids in that school, and current demographics dictate one in three will develop mental health issues, at some stage in their lives.

Probably all those kids possess a smart phone, Lee, as I expect you do yourself. I do as well, for the wealth of information they provide is invaluable.'

Lee disagreed, 'I only have a cheap old phone; it's not a smart phone, like yours.'

'Okay,' said the old man, 'but although I do have a smart phone it's a lot smarter than me, and smart phones can get you into trouble. For example, various government agencies record every text message and every call from these devices, even if they currently deny it, because it garners a wealth of information about the man in the street, from his shopping habits to his sexual peccadillos and infidelities. In point of fact, the real danger now is from the portable laptop, or I-Pad, which most teenagers possess, and use to access mainstream websites around the world.

When you look at the hundreds of kids down there, Lee, do you realise that many will have children and a good marriage, but most will not? A lot of the girls will be unable to have children, while one in three will have an abortion at some point in their lives, and statistically more than one, for currently the number of legally recorded abortions runs at one and a half thousand-million since nineteen-eighty, which equates to one for every woman on the planet. You can view the statistics in "real-time" by logging onto one of the numerous 'Abortion-Counter' sites, on the Web. I must tell you that many academics suspect the reason this world is in such a mess is the fact that for ages no real genius has surfaced with the intellect to enlighten the world. This used to occur every few decades; but the trouble now is all our little 'Einsteins' are being chopped up, before they get a chance to put in an appearance.'

'Wow,' exclaimed Lee, 'I guess that *is* possible … if you consider the massive numbers of illegal abortions, which could be a lot more!'

The old man continued. 'Others will be hungry for love and security, and may turn to prostitution. The chances are that quite a few of those children will take a life, intentionally or accidentally. Many will end their own lives by suicide or accidental overdoses. Some will exploit their strength or their sexuality, while others will be victims all their lives. At least a third will develop some form of cancer, and quite a few will inevitably become alcoholics and junkies, or even paedophiles, for all innocence is fleeting and surrenders to time; yet nobody sets out to become any of these things. The current education system really needs to do a lot more.'

'In what respect?' queried Lee.

'In educating the youth of today as to what they will encounter out there in the real world, regarding things like 'legal-highs', and social media, where terrorists recruit the vulnerable, and of course all the pornography they will see on the internet. As these children grow up and mature they will each evolve into the average of the people they mix with in life; and the things that those people do to them, and for them: and even what they make them do to themselves. Some will be relatively content but most will wallow in lonely lives of quiet desperation. Getting married or having a partner in life does not always alleviate loneliness, which like pain, afflicts us all at some point.

If someone seems happy all the time they are either stupid, selfish, or blind to the suffering that permeates the world. Most of them will cherish hopes and dreams searching all their lives for ultimate happiness, which of course, being perfection, is unattainable on this Earth.

Lee, do you realise that each and every one of those children down there possesses the potential to become the most wicked individual to ever walk the face of the Earth, or alternately, the greatest force for good that mankind has ever known? Evil is latent in us all, and to kill and torture is inherent in human nature, but many people believe the purpose of life is to rise above human nature. Everyone possesses an instinct for good and evil, so every child down there has the capacity for the greatest good, or the greatest evil. If you doubt mankind has evil within him, check out the profusion of torture devices used throughout history, and even in our current age.

But although tremendous evil exists there is always the balance of a spiritual dimension, where one may aspire to the kindest, noblest, most heroic qualities. However, bear in mind that good only comes to those who seek it, whereas evil lurks round every corner.'

'But tell me about the dangers of the internet?' interrupted Lee, who had never experienced it.

'Well, the horrific propaganda put out by terrorist groups ensnares young people and even radicalizes them to kill strangers and plant bombs. Witness the fourteen-year-old Manchester schoolboy, who became so radicalised by religious extremists on the internet, that he plotted to behead a police officer. That same year, in Syria, a boy of the same age betrayed his mother to ISIS when she begged him to flee the country. They got him to behead her, and use her head as a football.

Young people around the world are now being radicalised by the internet to commit atrocities. In July of twenty-sixteen, two nineteen-year-olds slit the throat of a priest in France, and beheaded him, as he was saying Mass; and earlier that month an ISIS suicide-group killed a score of foreigners in the capital of Bangladesh. What stunned that country most was the fact that those young Jihadists included university graduates. They all came from wealthy educated families; not from the poverty-stricken ghettos, which abound in that country. How can ISIS persuade people of that calibre to sacrifice themselves? In most of these events, even the immediate relatives have no inkling of the perpetrator's persuasion or dedication. Such commitment can never be conquered by logic, in my view!

Just before that, in America, a lone gunman killed fifty people in a nightclub; he was a young Jihadist, whose father followed ISIS and totally radicalised his own son, but he is the exception, because most Jihadi are so secretive, that their immediate family have no suspicion, when they commit an atrocity.

But bear in mind in mind that pornography is now a multi-billion-dollar internet industry, with tens of thousands of websites, where explicit videos of bizarre sexual habits and pastimes are broadcast worldwide to anyone who cares to look for them. I'm not suggesting everyone is particularly vulnerable, Lee, for we are not simply programmed robots, but neither are we super-beings!'

Lee concurred, 'I can certainly agree with that.'

'But in fact,' the old boy continued, 'you don't even have to search these things out. For example, if you simply log on to a dating agency on the Web, sooner or later things called Cookies are thrust onto your screen. They are supposed to be adverts, but are so insidious that if you close them down, they simply return when you go to the next page. You usually have to log off the internet, and actually close your computer down, to get rid of them. And if you haven't taken the care to erase the current history of what you last looked at, when you fire your computer up again they come straight back onto that little screen, which becomes the retina of your mind's eye. They may look interesting, but remember, curiosity killed the cat, and some of these sites record your interests and inject a 'Trojan-Horse' virus which, like the Greek legend, opens itself much later and copies all your contacts and e-mails. It may then forward the same virus to all the people you have ever contacted on your computer, since you first purchased the thing and you may even end up getting sexually blackmailed. This is now known as 'revenge-porn' or 'sexploitation.'

You may suddenly hear a voice as you surf the Web, but when you close your current page, a live video of some glamour-girl in her bedroom is there on your screen, talking to you personally, for your computer is now linked to hers. As you realise this is now a live video link, she will ask if you want to chat to her? These are the web-cam sites, known as chat-rooms, where thousands of women make money by linking up to some guy's computer, without his initial consent.'

'Well, ...' countered Lee, 'that's just freedom-of-speech, or video ... if you like!'

'Ah, ... but it's much more insidious than that. In fact, the internet has only become globally available in the last twenty years and the more that that technology evolves, the more remote we will become from our fellow-beings and from nature, and if you are out of touch with nature you are out of touch with God. Now some aspects of human nature, which kids were never aware of, and never looked for, are dangled right in front of them to the point where they may get drawn into bizarre practices, because young minds are naturally curious to learn.'

Now Lee had little clue as to what his friend was expounding, as he had never used the internet, and had no wish to do so.

'I must tell you, Lee,' said the old man, 'of an article which I read last week, in the supplement of a Sunday newspaper. It has emerged that some schoolchildren, as young as eight, have become addicted to pornography on the internet, via their access to mobile phones and computers.'

The old man then started to relate how women have always felt the need to be more empowered in a man's world, where even in today's modern world they are paid lower wages and in benighted countries often routinely raped, especially where civil strife is indigenous, or where a state of war rages.

'Now women, world-wide, have discovered there are different ways in which they may become equal or superior to a man. They could become part of a suicide mission, for example, but a far less extreme manner could simply be in sexual exploitation, because thanks to the media, women have now become aware of how rich and varied are the desires of the average man. They realise that sexual desire maintains the law of diminishing returns, dictating the more one strives for satisfaction, the deeper one needs to delve and explore.'

The old man continued, 'So this means that man, who keeps searching and experimenting for whatever he feels will satisfy his desires, may get drawn into all sorts of bizarre practices and fetishes.'

'Do you mean paedophilia and things like bestiality, or some form of sexual cannibalism?' queried Lee.

'No, ... those things are mostly mental aberrations, although in Germany, recently, websites promoting bestiality became so prolific that the government there was forced to re-instate an ancient law prohibiting sex with animals. Apparently these websites have encouraged a sharp rise in that type of incidence; but generally I'm just referring to fetishes, to which ordinary people can sometimes become addicted.'

'Like what?' asked Lee.

'Almost anything your mind can fantasize about, from high-heels to ear-rings; there are even websites catering for 'cigarette fetishes', so almost anything can become a fetish for a man, if he lets curiosity get the better of him.'

Lee was astonished. 'Smoking!' he exclaimed.

'Yes ... indeed,' claimed the old man, 'but the saddest thing on the internet now is the amount of suicide-sites, where viewers are shown and even encouraged to use various methods for taking their own lives. The commonest methods are described in graphic detail, but I personally feel suicide is the epitome of despair; a state that some souls reach, where they feel all help and hope has gone, and all faith in the future has disappeared. Suicide is the saddest aspect of any so-called civilisation.'

The old man continued. 'Men are always starting wars, and there is always war raging somewhere around the world, where women and children seem to suffer the most. I suspect most women resent men for this, and also the physical prowess many men wield to abuse their partners, which creates thousands of refuge centres for women, up and down the country. So it's understandable that a fair number of women may actually resent men; but this has hidden repercussions. Take, for example, the proliferation of same-sex marriages, and the rampant rise in radical feminism.

But when we do find the odd exception of a woman rising to the pinnacles of power, they are just as ruthless in starting wars, or ignoring hunger.

I firmly believe mankind has an instinct for good, and conversely, for evil. He may not be aware of it, but his conscience is, and he feels guilty. The more power an individual acquires in life the more selfish and guilty he becomes. "Power corrupts, and absolute power corrupts absolutely."

There are some exceptions to this rule, but generally speaking most men who indulge in masochism are men of power, who sense the deprivation of lesser mortals, which makes them feel very guilty. The media is full of revelations about judges and politicians, whose sexual peccadillos are exposed on a regular basis. Pride will subdue their senses until they seek sex again, when once more they will impulsively feel the need to be punished.'

'So,' countered Lee, 'is this purely a male reserve, to which man is susceptible?'

'Predominantly, but a few women do subscribe to it, for many relish the pain and injury they may inflict without repercussion, so they too can become addicted in their sadism.'

Lee asked, 'So ... women can become as cruel as men?'

The old man paused, 'Yes, even more so, in some cases. Especially if they've been in abusive relationships; they are human as well, after all. Sadly, femininity is no criterion for compassion!

A prime example ... that well-known Croatian lady, Jacine Jadresko, the millionaire daughter of a property developer spends a fortune travelling the world, hunting down and killing rare animals. She has killed lions, an endangered species, and bears, hanging their hides up as trophies. Her killing ambitions now include hippos and elephants.'

'How can anyone acquire such bloodlust?' Lee queried, in disbelief.

'Well, she was spawned in the vicious Croatian civil war, which killed tens of thousands, and that might explain her callous indifference to suffering and the sanctity of life.'

'Well, at least her breed is dying out,' exclaimed Lee.

'Unfortunately not,' responded the old man, 'for although she is a single mum she has a son of ten whom she hopes will emulate her killing spree. This woman is so twisted she even encourages her boy to shoot little robins through the neck, with his own rifle.'

'Wow, ... it sounds like 'ISIS' could really use *him*!'

'God forbid, but maybe some vigilante will hunt *her* down and hang *her* skin out to dry, for she is covered in tattoos and *her* hide would make a lovely collector's item. But being totally shameless, she revels in the profusion of hate-mail that she receives from around the world. She epitomises that old adage - of absolute power corrupting absolutely!'

'Just makes me wonder who the real animals are on this planet,' concluded Lee.

'Well, I suspect there is just a thin veneer between civilisation and anarchy, and without that veneer we would all possess a primitive carnal nature, harbouring blatant contempt for man and beast. Most people meander through life, blind to the bleak realities of hunger, homelessness and poverty. Not through choice, but because our society dictates that family, health and wealth must come first, before the despair of others can intrude.'

Lee bid his farewell to the old man and left the park, a little sadder, a little wiser, but a lot more disillusioned.

CHAPTER FIVE

As summer faded, the ground acquired a tawny apron, as dead leaves cast their crisp carpet of rust over hordes of twigs, littering the land with the rustle of decay. Lee sensed the approach of winter, and felt he couldn't work outdoors for much longer as biting winds now numbed him to the bone. He decided to look elsewhere for a different job in a warmer environment.

He went to the Job Centre but discovered that when a new job was posted there at nine in the morning it had to be taken down and listed as filled an hour later, because thousands of hopefuls would already have applied, in the short time the vacancy was posted.

So Lee tasked himself with touring the many hotels and restaurants in town, seeking work; any kind of work, at any kind of hours.

Within a few days he received a phone text asking him if he was interested in a position as a night porter, at a little hotel along the seafront. He went along for a casual interview, where the main concern was ... 'could he make sandwiches and use a vacuum cleaner.' He convinced them that his experience from a similar London position covered most of the tasks involved, so after being shown how to sign in late-night guests, he was assured that if his references from the council regarding his job in the park were forthcoming, the position would be guaranteed.

He was able to start his new job after handing a week's notice in at the park, but he felt it was the longest, coldest week of his life. He said goodbye to the café people but promised the old man he would visit him, as he would be relatively free during the coming days, for he would now be working nights.

In his new job he was taught how to serve drinks and manage the cash-register.

He was able to scoot round with the vacuum cleaner after midnight and, as the season had virtually finished, was not bothered by guests booking in late for most of them arrived during daylight hours.

One exception was when a young 'boy-band' had booked the penthouse after their gig in the Whiterock Theatre nearby. He was stunned by the invincible arrogance of these youths, who seemed to believe their own hyperbole. He was told by their manager not to admit the scores of groupies who clung to the shirt-tails of these kids, plying them with ornate homemade greeting cards dotted with love poems and phone numbers.

He was very busy that evening, for many of the groupies had been invited by the boys into the foyer as their guests, and there was nothing Lee could do about it.

As Lee was handed another bunch of cards from the cluster of fans at the main door which was now locked, he presented them to the boys. They simply laughed scornfully at the ornate devotions and pledges of undying love so painfully inscribed, and the front-man of the group told Lee to dump them all in the trash. Lee put them aside and continued serving the drinks and making sandwiches, but deliberately singled out this boy for special treatment. He picked on him because he was the one who had initiated all the scorn his comrades sustained, so Lee ignored him for the rest of the evening. While he was serving the others this boy would ask what had happened to his food order, or when was he going to get his drinks, which he'd ordered ages ago.

Lee explained to him, that he was doing his very best, but because he was so busy having to serve everyone in turn he would just have to be patient.

Well, he was patient for an hour or so, but gave up in the end and retired, soon followed by the rest of the group. Lee spent a few hours clearing up, washing dishes, vacuuming and laying the tables for breakfast, before settling down to read the beautiful cards that he had been asked to trash. They brought tears to his eyes and he wondered how the boys, who owed their fame and prosperity to these devoted fans, could dismiss them so callously.

He received some telephone calls from other fans hoping to be put through to the group, but was under strict orders, not to connect any callers. As he fiddled about with the ancient 'Dolls Eye' telephone exchange in his tiny office, he chanced to break into a long distance conversation, which the lead singer was making to the United States.

He was talking to a girl in California, telling her he didn't play very well that evening, and that the gig was rubbish. He said he needed a rest and she told him to visit her in California, where he could relax in her beach house in Malibu, and use her father's Ferrari.

Lee nibbled on a stale leftover sandwich and reflected on the irony of life. He decided that, in this cesspool of life, only cream and scum rise to the top. One bonus Lee had acquired in his new job was that there was no way management could determine just how much liquor had been dispensed from the various spirit bottles; so every evening, after his work was finished, he was able to indulge in a nightcap. His favourite tipple was what he called a BMW. This was a mixture of Baileys, Malibu and Whiskey, and after a couple of these he was able to grab a few hours' shuteye, but he had to suck a few mints to ensure the morning staff never picked up on this habit. One Saturday night after a busy evening Lee was very tired, and after supping his nightcap, had lain down on the sofa facing the reception desk.

He had checked the till, cleaned the toilets and carpets, and set the breakfast tables, so he quickly fell asleep. His phone alarm woke him at six, as usual, and he lit the huge grills ready for the early breakfasts. He made fresh coffee for the morning staff, but when he went to give the outside door-plate a quick polish, discovered he had forgotten to lock the huge revolving door. 'Must cut down on the BMWs,' he mused. The first day-staff to arrive were the chambermaids, followed by the breakfast chef.

Suddenly all hell broke loose as people came running up, asking Lee where all the silver cutlery was; Lee knew where it should have been, but it was conspicuous by its absence. The manager was called, as were the police.

Lee was confronted with a dilemma. The manager queried how someone could carry loads of silver from the kitchen past the reception office, where he was supposed to be stationed. Lee's blood went cold as he realised they must have passed right in front of him as they left, and seen him lying there, asleep on the sofa. If he had woken up he would probably have been stabbed, or worse.

However, as he was the main suspect, the police insisted they escort him back to his home, which they intended to search. Lee knew he wasn't guilty but remembered that when he'd started this job, months earlier, he had 'borrowed' a single set of cutlery for personal use, which would have the hotel insignia stamped on them, but he was not in possession of the hundreds of precious knives, forks and spoons that had gone missing.

When his home was searched, Lee was arrested and charged with stealing the entire missing cutlery. The police decided they had their man, and could produce some pieces in court, so charged him with the theft. This would quickly solve the case and the court would doubtlessly assume some accomplice had absconded with the rest of the goods, before the police had arrived at Lee's abode. Lee pleaded not guilty but the fact that he had previously been convicted of driving a stolen car, just months earlier led the jury to convict him and he was sent to prison for twelve months, and would now have to serve the extra six months from his suspended sentence. This meant that even with time off for good behaviour, Lee would be locked up for at least a year, and now sadly realised yet another year from his life was going to waste. He was allocated to Lewes prison, the main centre for all types of offenders in the south of England. He realised now that he would not see La-Lu for another year until he was released, and as neither of them could phone each other in prison also realised he would need his friend Tom to visit her, if there was to be any communication between them.

Lee was given the job, as most Chinese inmates were, of working in the laundry. It was not pleasant and he received a very meagre allowance for long hours in stifling conditions but he did settle in, being able to speak to the others in his mother tongue of Mandarin.

After he got a severe asthma attack he was taken to the hospital wing for a week, and then transferred to the kitchens.

While recuperating, he learnt some devastating news on the prison grapevine. His nemesis, Ping, was being transferred to Lewes that very week. It was with apprehension that he started working in the kitchens, for one of his duties was serving meals to all the prisoners, and he was bound to meet Ping at some point in the future.

It was not long before he did encounter him, queuing up with the others. Lee was behind some serving tables at the time, slicing up bread, so it was fortunate that he was holding a large knife when Ping approached and threatened him in Chinese, which the attentive guards could not decipher.

They had been warned to keep an eye on these two and were on alert, but Ping knew time was on his side, and he would be able to get to Lee, sooner or later.

They were in separate wings but on one occasion both were released into the exercise yard at the same time. This did not normally happen, but Ping had bribed an officer, a new recruit, who was unaware of the acrimony between them.

Lee did not realise Ping was in the yard and did not notice him lurking behind another group of prisoners. Ping had fashioned a 'shank' from a plastic toothbrush. It was sharpened into a point and when he came up behind Lee, he stabbed him repeatedly, in the back. Like birds fleeing a sudden noise, the nearby prisoners scattered as Lee fell to the ground. When officers ran up, Ping was no longer around, having made a hasty retreat.

The shank of the toothbrush was still buried in Lee when he was rushed to the hospital ward, having lost much blood and in a critical condition. He was so badly injured he had to be rushed to Brighton-General hospital by helicopter, or he would have died. He had to have a kidney removed, and was in intensive care for some weeks.

Back in the recovery ward in Lewes prison, Lee had to lie prone for several days, and his back went into spasm as a result. He was prescribed tablets of OxyContin, a potent form of morphine, to alleviate the excruciating pain, which fortunately cleared up when he was able to move again. In the tiny prison ward, he was cared for by a Chinese nurse, who informed him that Ping had been seconded in solitary confinement since the attack, but no prosecution would take place because none of the witnesses would testify. He also learnt that Ping was even angrier than before, for he was convinced that he had finished Lee off, and swore he would complete the job when he was released to 'general population'.

The good news was that Lee was now eligible for criminal injuries compensation, which could run into thousands of pounds.

Lee had a visit from a friend who had worked with him in the prison laundry and was informed that if he wanted to survive he had to take care of Ping, permanently. Lee was told that Ping had bribed the system to house him on the same block as Lee, and possibly on the same floor. Things didn't look good, but they decided on a simple method to dispose of this deadly problem.

Lee had to steal some hypodermic needles from the ward before he was moved, for his friend told him how to pierce the base of a light bulb so that it could be filled with petrol. When the bulb was ignited it would explode, showering flaming petrol everywhere.

Lee was told he would need two hollow needles so once he was able to get out of bed found a couple of used ones in a Sharps-Disposal container in the ward. He realised that one of the needles would get blocked as he methodically twisted it into the lead base of the bulb, which was why he would actually need two needles to complete the task.

In the hospital ward of the prison he was able to take as much time as he needed to do the job, as he was supposed to be immobilised in bed, and was not regarded as any sort of security risk. The rest was simple; he was able to use a standard light bulb, which his friend had procured from the laundry. He also managed to acquire a small container of petrol from one of the generators.

After successfully piercing the base of the bulb with one of the hypodermic needles, he carefully funnelled the fuel into it with the other clean needle, leaving the filament intact so it looked like there was just air inside. He sealed the tiny hole in the base and his friend secreted the bulb where nobody would ever look, under a machine, back in the laundry.

Sure enough, when Lee was released he discovered that Ping had been given a different cell, just yards away from his own. However, this suited his purpose, for they ignored each other and everybody thought things had quietened down.

Ping was fond of boxing and there was a big prize-fight one evening, down in the television lounge. Lee knew that Ping wouldn't miss it, as the prisoners were allowed to watch an hour or so of television, before overnight lockdown.

Lee had ground up a dozen of the OxyContin tablets, which he had hoarded from his recent stay in the ward. He waited until the other inmates left, to watch the boxing match on television, and then quaffed the lot with a swig of prison-brew alcohol. His timing had to be perfect for he realised he would shortly slip into a coma so, as he waited for all the cell doors to be opened, he carefully watched as Ping stomped out of his own cell. He then checked that the other cells on his landing were empty before sneaking into Ping's cell, carefully cradling the volatile light bulb. Lights in the cells were normally left on, as a matter of security, so he had to switch off the ceiling light and wait for it to cool before he could unscrew it.

He made a slight noise as he pulled the chair over to stand on, so froze for a moment, listening intently. All he noticed were shouts coming from the TV room so he quickly unscrewed the old bulb and carefully inserted the new one, making sure it wasn't leaking. He ensured everything was just as he found it before leaving the cell. He knew that once Ping tried to switch his light on, the voltage would cause the filament to glow red hot, igniting the petrol and making the bulb blow up.

He was already feeling drowsy as he made the way back to his own cell, where he stripped off and climbed into bed. He was out cold in a few minutes, and shortly afterwards slipped into a coma.

Soon the recreation time was up and, as the guards were anxious to get the inmates into their cells for the night, they were quickly led back as the head officer waited impatiently by the gate buttons, which locked all the cell doors for the duration of the night.

Ping glared into Lee's cell as he passed, but Lee was in bed, fast asleep. When he entered his own cell he was surprised to find it in darkness. As he went over to check the bulb his cell door closed, so he just tried the light switch. He was surprised to see the bulb glow but give out no light. As he stood looking up at it in wonder, the thing exploded in his face, blinding him and setting his clothes on fire.

Before anyone knew what was happening the fire alarms went off but before they could open the cell doors to rescue Ping, he was burned to a cinder. Lee remained in bed as a general evacuation was called, but he had to be dragged out, for the guards could not wake him. He was rushed to the infirmary, when they realised he had overdosed in what seemed an obvious suicide attempt. The authorities had too many suspects to isolate anyone specific, as Ping had many enemies in the prison. Besides, their sympathies lay with Lee, who was unconscious at the time, so Ping's death was not exactly given top priority.

When Lee was released a few months later, on compassionate grounds, he was housed back in his old flat in the tower block where he found he was blessed with a new neighbour. She was an elderly lady who seemed very friendly and peaceful, but she owned a dog; a mini-schnauzer. Lee wasn't too concerned, for the dog seemed similar in character to its owner. Besides, he was preoccupied by the imminent hearing of his Criminal Injuries tribunal. It was scheduled in a week's time when his claim would be assessed, and he had been informed he would be eligible for a substantial pay-out.

CHAPTER SIX

Later that weekend, the elderly neighbour who owned the little dog invited Lee to tea. He was initially reluctant, as dogs were anathema to him, but then decided he should make an effort to get on with his neighbour. They had a very pleasant conversation as each exchanged a history of their various ailments. She seemed concerned when she learned that Lee had recently lost a kidney when, as he told her, he fell off a ladder.

She mentioned that she had recently had a 'pre-op' for a hysterectomy and was slightly concerned because of her age, yet seemed more worried about the dog's welfare than her own.

However, she told him all the latest gossip about the refuse collections and other details, in which Lee endeavoured to show interest. She then told Lee she had been careful to purchase her little dog from a family, for everyone told her how important it was to check that a puppy came from a family environment and not a dog farm, where mother dogs were repeatedly kept pregnant in atrocious, filthy conditions. That way they could just be bred over and over again, with each of the pups sold in a matter of weeks, generating lots of income at five hundred pounds each. Unfortunately, she found out later, through the dog's papers, that the mother dog she had seen her pup with was just a beautiful example of that particular breed, simply being passed around a network of breeders, who fooled buyers into thinking that this was her first litter, whereas none of the pups she was with were in fact her own.

After indulging in a couple of gins together, they parted company and Lee returned to the solace of his television.

He made sure to keep the noise down, for he knew the old lady retired early, as he always heard her taking the dog out early in the morning.

Lee's case was heard later that week, and he was delirious when the court awarded him substantial damages for his injuries. Twenty thousand pounds: a tidy sum.

He realised this could set La-Lu and himself up for a future life together, and resolved not to spend it except for emergencies.

He need not have worried, for now a host of credit cards came fluttering through his door. Before this award he could not get an overdraft, never mind a loan from his bank, but now that he didn't need the money, offers of credit simply flooded in. He decided to take some up on their offers, for he might need reserves to fall back on in the future.

Tom rang one evening and told Lee he had kept in touch with La-Lu in Holloway, visiting on a number of occasions. Lee was very grateful for this, as it had been the only way of relaying information between them, at a time when he and La-Lu had both been in prison. He arranged with Tom to visit her as soon as possible.

However, Lee was asleep that night when he awoke to cries coming from his neighbour's bedroom. He ran to her flat, and in panic, smashed down the front door. The little dog was whining, and the old lady was deathly pale, so an ambulance was immediately called. Before she was carted off on a stretcher she made Lee promise to look after the dog until her return. She told him her little dog always sensed when she was ill, before she even realised it herself. Also ... she told Lee, that she firmly believed dogs and cats possessed gifts of extra-sensory-perception, and could even detect cancer in humans.

Lee stuck to his word, and reluctantly took the dog into his own flat after feeding it. He figured that although he was banned from owning a dog, officially he could look after one, and anyway, who would find out?

Lee expected the old lady to return home in a few days, but he had to walk the dog and allow it to sleep in his own flat. He had to move its bed and feeding bowls into his kitchen, and was forced to walk the creature in the park, where the other dog walkers were astounded to see Lee with a dog of his own.

They all became sympathetic when they heard the reason, and he was inundated by offers of help and advice. After a day or so he quite looked forward to the walks in the park, where he would meet the others who were concerned for the welfare of both him and the dog, and of course, the old lady.

Lee played with a tennis ball that the dog had found, and was surprised how much fun he was having in the company of this dog. In fact, when it once ran off he became very anxious until someone brought it back to the café, and they were reunited.

But a few days later, he was shocked when the police called on him early one morning, informing him that the old lady had died during the night from an abdominal aortic aneurism.

The dog was now sleeping in a corner of Lee's bedroom, where he had placed an old blanket over its basket. The little dog would pull this up over its head when it wanted to sleep. It would waken Lee every morning by placing its legs on the edge of his bed, and gently tapping his nose with a little paw until he opened his eyes. Lee now realised that he either had to take the dog on as a permanent fixture or get it put down, as the old lady had no relatives.

The dog was now used to Lee and the layout of the flat and even the building, so they became very attached to each other. When Lee wanted to lie down for a siesta in the afternoon the dog waited until he fell asleep, before hopping up on the bed. Lee would find the creature resting its little head on his chest when he awoke and decided there was no way he was going to abandon his new friend. He was surprised how faithful the dog was, and how it would follow him everywhere and even wait patiently outside a shop when he went in to buy something.

One day he went into a shop for cigarettes, but when he came out the dog had gone. He hadn't tied it up, so felt someone may have stolen it. He hung around for a while quizzing passers-by but nobody had seen anything. He then went to the park café, hoping the dog had perhaps gone there in search of him.

At the café he was told by Lucy, one of the regulars, that a series of dog thefts had recently occurred in Hastings and that small, feisty dogs were the thieves' favourites because they were sacrificed to train fighting dogs, like bull terriers. Dog fighting was something Lee never knew existed, and he was horrified to learn when he phoned Tom, that little dogs were the dog-nappers' preference as they could be used as bait, putting up a good fight, but inevitably being torn to pieces by bigger animals. The dog thieves were careful not to steal any dogs that might damage their own precious dogs, but only ones that could put up some resistance, but not too much.

Lucy advised him to advertise his missing pet by putting posters on lamp-posts, offering a large reward for the dog's safe return. He had plenty of money from his recent award, so he offered a thousand pounds for any information leading to the dog's recovery.

Days passed until one evening he received a phone call from two girls who claimed they knew someone who had taken the dog, and if they were able to rescue it, would they still get the reward?

Lee agreed without hesitation and arranged to meet them that very evening in the park. He was there early, with the money in cash, and was surprised when a top-of-the-range Land Rover pulled up in the car park. Two girls jumped out and approached him. He queried where the dog was, but the girls told him they first needed some money for expenses. After some haggling, when it was agreed that Lee would hand over five hundred pounds, the two girls promised to fetch the dog immediately. They told Lee that the thieves had gone to the pub, leaving the dog in a kennel, where they could easily rescue it.

Lee realised that if they did have his dog they wouldn't get another five hundred for selling him, and as they had seen the colour of his money, they knew they could only benefit by returning the animal. Sure enough, half-an-hour later, when it was dark, the same vehicle pulled into the car park and out jumped the dog with the two girls. The rest of the money was handed over, but Lee, noticing two men in the back of the vehicle, headed off in a different direction.

The dog was delighted to see him, and didn't seem any the worse for wear. The next day Lee brought the dog to be micro-chipped and fitted with a tag inscribed with his phone number and the dog's name.

Lee had rung Tom, who lived some distance away, and told him the good news. He asked him if he would mind taking the dog with them on their visit to La-Lu, and Tom made no objection. They decided to go as soon as the visiting orders came through but, on past experience, realised this would take a number of weeks.

That evening Lee walked the dog along the seafront, where he would often pause outside a house with bright lights, giving him a glimpse into another world. He knew the people inside could not see him in the darkness, for he was able to stand in the shadows and watch as they cooked, ate and watched television. He would often hover in the darkness, watching these scenarios in silence and sadness, with the little dog sitting patiently by his feet. He was always amazed by the loyalty, affection and trust that the little dog displayed, but it made him cringe with guilt, in memory of the old days in China, when he so cruelly mistreated these animals in the markets.

That was a different time, a time when he had felt no pity, or compassion, or mercy for any living thing. He had never realised that animals could actually become faithful companions, sharing love with their human guardians, even defending them to the death. He now understood why dogs are called 'man's best friend'.

As they walked on the beach Lee Fong looked out to sea. Somewhere out there was his homeland, to where he hoped one day to return, but right now his life was a mess, and he was in turmoil. He sat on the windy beach with the dog, as his feelings ebbed and flowed like the waves cascading on the shingle. They made the very ground vibrate, as the wind whipped cascades of spray from their crests, before they crashed down in torrents of foaming fury.

As he gazed out at the dark depths, he reflected how a young girl had drowned at this very spot, just weeks ago, and reflected how ephemeral and erratic life had become.

He wondered about the girl's family, and her friends and the grief they must have felt when her body was washed ashore. Probably guilt as well as grief, as these emotions often went hand in hand, as Lee could readily testify.

But these were things that one had to come to terms with, being part and parcel of life itself.

He knew he was still a simple Chinaman, who spoke little and smiled less, not that he had much to smile about, but the little dog accepted him for what he was. The dog was now tired and had stretched out to sleep on the beach, oblivious to the roar of the ocean.

Even when he strolled along here during the day, as the sunshine lent crystalline beauty to the translucent shades of the waves, he never felt accepted or acknowledged. He would watch young families playing with their children on the beach, and try in vain to remember his own childhood, but could not, which he reflected was maybe a blessing.

In China his own parents already had their allocation of one child, so when Lee was born the authorities immediately took him away to the orphanage, where he grew up with Ping and La-Lu.

In England he was always conscious of being a foreigner, an immigrant, and one to be wary of. It may have been the pain etched in his face, or the grim set of his jaw, but since his arrival in the country years ago, he noticed people seemed to avert their gaze when he glanced at them. It was many months before he realised they found him menacing, sensing that he was different, in the way the seagulls flying above seemed different to the other birds; and often viewed as a threat.

But surely, he thought, everyone was the same. He even regarded Ping as his family, for they had been brought up as children in the same home. And wasn't everyone his family; surely we all spring from the same origins. We all possess the same common heritage, proving we are all brothers and sisters, related one to another. Certainly, we all possess the same fears, the same weaknesses, the same desires and the same hunger. After all, every entity shares the same propensities ... eating, sleeping, mating and defending. They hope for nothing less than the chance to live out their lives with purpose and fulfilment, garnering whatever satisfaction and happiness they can.

Of course, Lee also felt those needs but found little love or purpose in his own life, apart from the little dog lying asleep at his feet.

He was, he admitted, afraid of death. Not dying, but death itself, and the finality of endless blackness. Even his little dog fared better in that respect, for it had no fear or knowledge of death, unlike Lee who was an expert on the subject.

The dog had started causing problems with its boisterous nature. When Lee took it to the park, it latched onto any tennis balls it spotted, and was soon capturing them from other dogs. One of these owners followed Lee for over a mile, waiting for him to retrieve the ball, which his little schnauzer had snatched from the other dog. Lee sensed the owner was quite upset and wasn't going to give up, but neither was the little schnauzer. The harder Lee chased him and the louder he shouted, the more the little rascal scampered away. Lee offered the man some money to compensate for his loss, but the guy was having none of it; he just wanted the ball back, and was growing more aggressive by the minute. Eventually they both cornered the culprit by the riverbank and the stranger retrieved his tennis ball; and not a minute too soon.

Lee retreated to the café, where he related the incident to the others. Somebody suggested he purchase a radio-collar, used to train dogs that misbehaved.

Lee learned that this gadget comprised two sections: A collar which fitted around the dog's neck, and a tiny radio transmitter, which he could carry in his pocket. Apparently there were a number of settings on the device, and initially a tiny buzzer vibrated against the dog's neck to let him consider the fact that this vibration would soon be followed by a mild electric shock, if it didn't stop what it was doing.

Lee was reluctant to consider the gadget until one of the other dog owners explained he had used one himself on his own dog and it worked really well, for his dog had now stopped barking at others. He no longer needed the device, so Lee bought it from him for a bargain price and it seemed to work well, although he found its range was rather limited.

However, it proved effective for soon the schnauzer realised the buzzer was a warning, and Lee had only to buzz once or twice for it to drop anything it had seized from another dog. However, at the café some days later, his dog could not resist grabbing a ball from another visitor. Lee pressed the buzzer, but it didn't work, for the dog had run round the side of the café, out of range. Now the dog realised that if it ran fast enough it could escape any repercussions, as the collar wouldn't work and there was nothing to worry about.

Sadly, this backfired when the schnauzer grabbed a sausage given to another dog, and quickly ran off before Lee could grab the transmitter. Unfortunately, it decided to run across the road adjoining the café, to escape any shock from the collar, and to Lee's horror a sudden sound of squealing tyres told him his dog had been run over.

When everyone ran to the spot, it was obvious there was nothing they could do. Lee held the dog tenderly, until it slowly expired in his arms, and everyone was heartbroken.

Death was a regular visitor in Lee's life, but he never got used to it. He had seen it and caused it, most of his life, and it showed. He now felt bitter and sad, almost betrayed by the gods. Ever since the orphanage days he accepted that peer pressure dictated real men never cried, so, although he desperately wanted to weep, he stiffened his resolve and stifled his emotions.

Now, when he awakened in the mornings, the only thing that made him get up was the curiosity of what possible ironies would befall him that day.

Lee had been incarcerated for the winter and most of the spring. But, as summer rolled around again, Lee's world warmed up. Sadly, the little dog was absent. He missed it patting his nose to wake him up; and he missed it lying across his chest: and he missed taking it for walks.

However, Tom visited Lee a few days later, informing him the visiting orders had arrived, so early the next day they headed up the motorway to London, and Holloway prison. La-Lu knew they were coming, for Tom had arranged the visit, so they didn't expect any trouble.

On arrival they quickly found a spot in the car park, and were heralded into the waiting room. Tom went in first to see La-Lu as Lee took time to compose himself, wondering just what to tell her. A lot had happened since they last met, and since his early release she did not know about the dog, and had not expected to see him so soon.

Tom returned with a beaming smile, and ushered Lee in on his own. La-Lu looked completely different to when he saw her last. She had regained weight, and seemed radiant. Her eyes shone and she smiled brightly at him. He simply fell in love with her, all over again. This was the old La-Lu he had grown up with, in China. He thought she must have been granted an early release, but that was not the case. She asked him to sit down, and listen to her without interruption.

She explained, 'Tom has been witnessing to me, during his recent visits. You know he found God and wanted to share this with me. To start with, this irritated me, but I humoured him, for he was the only visitor I ever got in this place. He claimed he was now a Christian, a follower of Christ, whom he told me was the human side of God, sent on Earth to save sinners. I didn't even believe in God, and I didn't know this Christ figure, although I did realise I was a sinner.

But to me it was all a delusion, generated by loneliness and a need to believe in something after death. The only book I was ever allowed to read in here was the Bible, and I never really bothered looking at it for it seemed so irrelevant in this modern world.

Well, something happened. I got into a bad situation with another inmate, who was supplying me with heroin, but when she realised she was going to get her cell searched, she asked me to hide her large stash of drugs.

I took it, but I couldn't resist the temptation to shoot the whole lot into me. I overdosed but everyone knew what I had done. I was rushed to the medical wing, but recovered, and she was waiting for me when I got out. She told me I had to pay back, or pay the price. She was going to cut me up, if I didn't deliver and I couldn't see a way out. She had done this to others in here, using two razor blades taped together, and held apart by matchsticks wedged between them.

When you get slashed on the face with this, you are not just left with a deep cut, but a thin slice of skin has to be removed, as they cannot stitch this tiny sliver on both sides. This leaves a thick permanent scar on your face for the rest of your life.

I had hit rock bottom. My life was in danger, and as I went to bed that night, I prayed to this God to show me a way out. I flicked open the Bible at random, closed my eyes, and put my finger on a line. Believe it or not, but the very sentence I read told me that I would be helped if I just put my trust in this God.

The strange thing is, Lee, the next day this woman was transferred to a different prison, because they searched her in the courtyard and found the very weapon she was going to use on me. Now every time, when I am in trouble, I do the same thing. I close my eyes, pick up the Bible, which is sometimes lying upside down and stick my finger in amongst the pages, on a random spot, and read the passage next to it. I found out later that this habit is known as *Dipping*.

It always guides me, but it also showed me that some force was aware of my problems, and what could this be, apart from the living God. I started meeting other Christians in here, who introduced me to the Pastor, who helped me accept Christ as my Saviour. And then, when I confessed my sins I no longer felt the need for heroin, which I've been hooked on for ten years. I don't need to inject any more, and feel no desire to even smoke it, so I guess some sort of miracle happened to me.'

Lee was speechless. He didn't know what to say. Here was his lifelong friend who not only smuggled heroin but got badly addicted to it, ending up in jail, now confessing she had found religion and faith in a God that he adamantly refused to believe in.

On the journey back Lee was unhappy with his friend. 'What have you done to her,' he demanded, 'she's like a different person. I don't even know her. I can never relate to all that rubbish.'

'I haven't changed her, God has,' responded Tom, 'but you are right. Now she is a different person.'

Lee retorted, 'How can anyone believe in something that has no beginning, or no end. It just doesn't make sense.'

'What time is it, Lee?' asked Tom, changing the subject.

'I dunno,' said Lee, 'I don't even have a watch.'

'Ah, … but you do believe in time?' queried Tom.

'What are you on about now?' said Lee.

'Well, … time itself has no beginning and no end.'

'So what,' said Lee. 'That doesn't prove there's a God.'

'But other things exist, which have no beginning, or end,' said Tom.

'Like what?' queried Lee.

'Well, space … to start with. If you travelled straight up in a rocket and kept going in a straight line, where would you end up?'

'At the end of space, I suppose; the perimeter!'

'So, what lies beyond that?' asked Tom.

'Never been there; wouldn't know: infinity, I suppose,' said Lee.

'Okay, …' said Tom. 'I can give you something else to think about. Take numbers, for example. There is no largest number that you can count to - even on a computer; and of course, you can always put another decimal point before even the smallest number.

Now! ... there are three examples you can accept as having no start and no end. The concept of God is simply another analogy, and many physicists believe there may be other dimensions, which we cannot sense.'

'What sort of dimensions?' queried Lee.

'Spiritual ones, and the supposition of a multiverse, as opposed to the universe, ... and things like black-holes, and supernovas!'

'What do you mean?' asked Lee.

'Well, ... have you any idea how big the universe really is, or your place in it?' asked Tom.

Lee responded, 'I know we're in a corner of a galaxy called the Milky Way.'

'Correct,' said Tom. 'But did you know every element on Earth was formed by the heat of the stars, which all owe their light to nuclear fusion. You see, after the 'Big Bang' temperatures reached one hundred-million-trillion-trillion degrees, causing the universe to start expanding, which it's still doing.'

Lee queried. 'Oh, really! Centigrade, or Fahrenheit?'

'It's irrelevant,' said Tom, 'because that's so hot it doesn't make any difference. That temperature is like the figure ten, with a few dozen zeros after it !

But,' he continued, 'I must tell you, Lee, ... science now accepts that infinite particles from this Big Bang clustered together to form different fusion reactions, and as all the dust grounded together, stars were formed that varied in density, according to the gravity exerted on them. Most of them formed within them lighter elements like hydrogen, but some got so dense they imploded into supernovas, producing all the other elements, like iron. This means that everything on Earth and indeed the universe, originated from the dust of stars; so basically we are all stardust, as the philosopher Plato claimed.'

Lee retorted. 'If we're all made from stardust, that means God didn't make us after all.'

Tom elaborated. 'But, ... don't you see, Lee, no matter how we originated, or where we came from, God must have started the whole process. It even says in 'Psalms' that ... "I knew you before you were formed", so where were we, for God to know us before our birth, and in the Gospel of John, our Lord claimed ... *"I have other sheep, which are not of this fold".'*

'So,' queried Lee, 'where might they be?'

'Heaven only knows,' Tom cryptically replied, 'but do you know that in the Milky Way alone, there are four-hundred-billion stars, and we inhabit only one of the hundred-billion planets revolving round them. In fact, our galaxy is over a hundred and twenty-thousand light-years across, and only one of a hundred-thousand-million galaxies that we know about?'

'What exactly is a light-year, then?' Lee asked.

'It's the distance light travels in the period of one year, going at a hundred and eighty-six-thousand miles-a-second.'

'And how far is that in miles?' queried Lee.

'About six trillion, or if you like, six-million-million!'

'And that's just one light-year! So, to get across our own galaxy at that speed would take us a hundred and twenty thousand years!'

'Yes,' Tom continued, 'but scientists have proved that in outer space worm-holes exist, which can warp the space-time continuum. It is now theoretically possible to travel through space, much faster than light, if we can find ways of utilising these worm-holes. Also, it's been proved that billions of minute particles from the Sun, called neutrinos, travel through our Earth and ourselves, every second. And let's not forget the enigma of dark-matter, which comprises most of the universe. In fact, in the last century a poor Indian named Ramanujan, who unfortunately died very young, is now seen as possibly the greatest mathematical genius the world has ever known. He turned science upside down with his ideas regarding black-holes; but he once said, "An equation is meaningless to me, unless it expresses a thought of God," – but I don't believe we have all the answers yet.'

Lee now felt that he didn't have any of the answers, except that there couldn't be a God, or he must be a total sadist. The rest of the journey home was spent in subdued silence.

CHAPTER SEVEN

Lee contacted La-Lu after recovering from her news, and soon realised she really had changed. She told him she now prayed for him every day, and more so, prayed most of the day. It seemed to Lee she had been brainwashed and become a religious fanatic.

Lee found himself sliding into depression. He did not even realise it until he had to go to his doctor for insomnia. He was prescribed some strong tablets to help him sleep.

Two things happened. Lee found, after a few days on these tablets, that he couldn't get up until the middle of the day. He also got addicted to them so badly, that if he didn't take them he couldn't get to sleep at all. He went to the doctor for more advice and she advised him to pursue some outdoor hobby, like golf, or horse riding.

He wasn't into golf but he had enough money to go to a riding school. It was expensive, but now he was beginning to relate to animals more than ever. As he was a complete novice, he was assigned an ageing, gentle creature, and this particular horse was allocated for him every time he turned up. He got to love this beast, once he got over his initial nervousness, and learned to canter, and then gallop.

Summer was drawing to a close as Lee found himself riding alone, out in the wilds; through the leafy woods and the deep valleys. This took his mind off La-Lu, but every night he would think of her before going to sleep.

In her last letter he had received devastating news. Firstly, she told him that she might be eligible for early release, but then explained the reason why. She had developed cancer, but didn't go into details.

Apparently, because of this, she was permitted visits from some nuns who resided at a nearby convent and was told that God had a call upon her life. She now felt she had a vocation and that the discipline and seclusion of a religious order was what she really wanted.

It had been agreed at her parole hearing that if she committed herself to this order and took religious vows, she could spend the rest of her sentence in the convent, instead of prison. In her letter she gently explained that any plans they had made in the past would have to be abandoned as she now yearned for a solitary life, without any male companionship.

Lee simply could not believe this state of affairs, and was deeply shocked. His depression returned with a vengeance when he realised La-Lu was no longer in his life for she had always given him a reason to carry on and plan for the future, but now there was nothing, and nobody.

He took to his bed, and spent most of the time watching old movies. He would watch three or four a day, which suited him fine, as it was a great escape from current realities.

The one thing he did continue to pursue was his horse riding. He also purchased a newspaper every day, as this not only helped his English, but kept him in touch with the world.

He no longer used his mobile as the battery had expired and would not take a charge any more. So Lee retreated into a little world of his own, until one day he read something, which upset him greatly.

He read about a nearby farmer, who had abandoned some donkeys in a quarry. Apparently, when they were discovered wallowing in a quagmire, with grossly overgrown hooves and badly emaciated flesh, they all had to be destroyed.

The farmer appeared in Court, later that week, and was found guilty of animal cruelty and fined five hundred pounds.

Lee became incensed, for he had met this farmer who hired horses out to his local riding school. Indeed, he owned a large farm next to the school. Lee realised that five hundred pounds was a paltry sum to such a person, and decided that this man should be taught a lesson.

So, next time he hired his horse out he equipped himself with a tin of brake fluid. The idea was to cover the farmer's Range Rover with it, for he knew from experience this stuff would not just destroy the paintwork but would eat into the metal bodywork of the vehicle.

He knew which car the man drove, and what days he normally visited the school.

The farmer was at the riding stables when Lee arrived, and so was his car. Lee hired out his favourite animal and rode down the lanes to where the farm was situated. Horse riders used this track on occasion, so nobody would find his appearance out of place. Lee's old horse trotted briskly along, beneath the forest canopy, which now shed its rustic carpet on twig-laden pathways. The creature cantered along the trail, now bounded by skirts of heathland, where fallow fields hinted at ripening suburbia. From the thinning undergrowth, birds dipped and dived between bushes, darting bravely past the horse's steaming head, tempting fate. As the trees thinned, the forest floor eased from rafts of leaves to open pasture, where Lee suddenly spied the farm, nestling by the brow of a hill.

He tethered his horse to a clump of trees and settled down to await the farmer's return. The wind was rising now, and Lee was pleased he had remembered his warm scarf, and of course gloves, to avoid leaving possible fingerprints at the scene.

He figured he would have to wait some time, so decided to have a quick look around. He knew he would hear the huge Range Rover bumping down the lane, as the farmer returned, so wasn't too worried about being caught on the property.

He wandered into the barn, which was full of hay bales, which he decided to put a light to, for this would be better than damaging the car. He dropped a lit match onto the hay and it ignited immediately. Just as he was leaving the barn he spotted something lying in the corner. It was a rusty old shotgun. He picked it up and noticed some shells nearby. It seemed an ancient weapon, but Lee decided to walk off with it under his coat. It would teach the old bastard right if he stole it. He put a shell into the gun and decided it might even work, if he cleaned it up.

As he was leaving the farm he suddenly spotted the farmer running towards him. He discovered later that the Range Rover had failed to start so the farmer had borrowed a bicycle from the stables, which was why Lee had not heard his approach.

The farmer recognised Lee and realised he must have set the hay bales alight. He shouted out that Lee was under arrest and that he was taking him to the police. He looked round for his shotgun, which suddenly appeared in Lee's hands. Everything seemed to happen at once. The farmer made a run for Lee, who panicked and tried to defend himself with the gun barrel, but it went off, and blew the farmer to the ground. As Lee dropped the weapon the wooden barn caught fire. He did not need to check if the farmer was merely injured, for one look at the body confirmed there was no chance of anyone surviving such a blast at close range.

As he fled the scene, Lee was relieved to see his placid horse had remained nearby, despite the flames, which were now roaring with intensity. He quickly got back on the horse and galloped to where the stable personnel were gazing at the glow on the hill.

'Must be a fire up there on the farm,' assumed one of the crowd.

'No idea,' claimed Lee, 'I've been in the forest all afternoon.'

'You're sweating, and so is your horse. You must have had a good ride,' said the manager. Lee paid his dues and went on his way, noting a convoy of fire engines heading past him on their way to the scene.

Lee decided he must maintain his usual routine, which meant going to the café to meet up with the other dog lovers.

He later teamed up with Lucy and the animal rights activists who applauded the unknown hero who had exacted vengeance on the cruel farmer. They loved the irony that the farmer had been shot with his own gun, because they told Lee that he had used this to fire on their group, when they broke into his farm last Christmas, freeing fifty turkeys destined for slaughter.

The subject quickly changed to a recent incident, where a young schoolboy had been charged with animal cruelty. He was found kicking a small sack, up and down the street where he lived, in a remote village in the country.

Apparently, he had been presented with a puppy as a Christmas present, and although he had begged his parents for one, found the routine of walking and feeding it just too much to handle. He had tied the tiny creature in a sack, and proceeded to use it a football, kicking it up and down the street. A neighbour noticed blood oozing from the sack and called the police. As the boy was under age they could not bring any charges, which incensed the community. It looked like the lad had got off scot-free, and his parents were more ashamed than he was over the resultant publicity.

The activists all agreed that someone should teach the boy a lesson and give him a good hiding. Lee decided there and then that he was the man for the job, but he kept this to himself.

Other matters seemed more pressing. He had received a letter from La-Lu, stating that she wanted to see him before she entered the convent. He managed to arrange a lift with Tom who had appealed to the authorities about an urgent visit. They agreed that he and Lee could visit the next day, because La-Lu would be entering the convent later that week. Tom had retired the previous week from his counselling job and had few other commitments.

The journey was uneventful and Lee avoided raising the subject of the farm, although Tom enquired if he was still taking riding lessons at the school. He told Lee he had booked him into an evening class, which would help his English and teach him about computers. To keep in his good books, Lee reluctantly agreed to this proposal, even promising to accompany Tom to church the following Sunday.

At the prison, Tom went in to see La-Lu first. He stayed only briefly, so that Lee could spend as much time with her as possible.

La-Lu seemed happy, despite being saddened by news of the dog. Lee dared not tell her about the farmer. Now she had religion, he didn't know if she would confess this to the authorities. She certainly had changed. She wore no make-up, and dressed very simply, even though the prison now allowed her to wear whatever clothes she wanted. She informed Lee that this was their last meeting at the prison, and she would be unable to receive any visitors at the convent until she had taken her final vows. She also told him she had become a vegetarian, and intended to lead a very simple life, devoted mainly to prayer.

She told Lee that when she was being prayed for recently, she had received the gift of the Holy Spirit, and had started to speak in 'tongues'. She also claimed her cancer tumour had apparently disappeared. Lee hadn't a clue what she was on about, but as time was precious he did not confront her on the matter.

Lee didn't understand the logic of any of it, for back home in China very few believed in God, and organised religion was banned. Even possession of a Bible would result in a prison sentence.

La-Lu was delighted to hear from Tom that Lee had agreed to go to church, but Lee wasn't as ecstatic as she was over the prospect.

On the journey home he had other matters on his mind. Principally, he wanted to visit the village where the boy who slaughtered the dog lived, to see what could be done to stop similar incidences happening in the future. In fact, he had no idea what he was going to do when he got there, except that he was determined to do something, even if he only lectured the lad on the error of his ways.

It was easy to find out where the dog had been killed as all the papers carried the story. The boy's name was withheld as he was under age, apparently under ten years old, but to Lee's mind still capable of evil.

A couple of days later Lee took a bus to the village where the incident took place. He went into the local pub and bought a pint of beer. After chatting to the locals, the name of the 'little bastard' surfaced, as he already had a fearsome reputation in the area. He was infamous for rampaging through gardens at night, and chucking eggs at windows, as the neighbours watched television.

Lee even discovered where he lived, and wandered round to see if he could spot the boy, for he had picked up a good description of the lad from locals in the pub.

As luck would have it, the house seemed deserted but he did spot someone climbing over the rear fence, leading to the nearby towpath. He instantly recognised the stocky kid with the bright red hair, so he scuttled up a nearby alleyway to confront him. The boy was walking on the canal towpath, and was approaching, when Lee stepped out in front of him.

'I want a word with you, young man,' he declared.

'Just piss off, you old scroat,' retorted the lad. Lee got angry, and grabbed the kid by the collar.

'You can't touch me,' he squealed. 'I'll have you done for child abuse.'

Lee knew that you could now be locked up if you manhandled a minor, and the offence-label on your cell door would read, 'Child Abuse'.

But Lee was infuriated. 'Touch you,' he cried, 'I'll break your bloody neck, you little bastard.'

The boy struggled violently to escape Lee's grasp, but in doing so, stumbled backwards into the canal. Lee couldn't swim, but apparently neither could the boy. Lee watched horrified as the current swept him away and stared helplessly as the child was dragged under. He decided there was nothing he could do, and ran off, grateful there were no witnesses about.

He read in the paper, some days later, of the tragic accident of a young boy who had drowned in a canal beside his house. In their search for the boy police dredged the nearby canal and found his body, and a mountain bike close by, with his DNA on it. They assumed the boy had accidentally ridden off the towpath, so recorded the case as a tragic accident. Lee now realised, with some shock, that he was responsible for the deaths of three individuals, directly, or indirectly, and he was far from happy about it.

CHAPTER EIGHT

Sunday came round, and Lee felt he must try to redeem himself and strive to be a better person, so decided that he really ought to accompany Tom to church. He listened in anticipation as Tom explained that this was a radically different kind of church, which he now attended.

The service was nearly two hours long and was full of 'happy-clappy' songs rather than hymns. A live group of musicians on the stage, rather than a traditional organ or piano, played these songs at 'pop-concert' levels, as massive speakers vibrated the very walls. Although the kids were herded into a crèche after the singing, the older youngsters still distracted Lee with the flickering screens of their mobiles and consoles, which they seemed to play right through the service. These are tolerated in churches these days as most people use their mobiles to download various scriptures, but Lee noticed that most of the teenagers were more interested in playing console-games, and texting people on their mobiles!

That was the first shock, but Lee was stunned to see how austere this converted warehouse seemed, as compared to the candlelit veneration of the old church, where he first went with Tom. He saw no statues or Icons here, and although Tom had explained these things were mere images, Lee noticed that these people seemed to harbour the prevailing aversion to Statues and Icons, that radical Jihadists fervently nurture.

There were no long wooden pews; just rows of plastic chairs and he saw no baptism font, or pulpit, or candlelit altar. In fact, what disturbed Lee most was the obvious absence of any crucifix, or even a cross.

Although he felt greatly inspired by this spirit-filled venue, learning that even hardened reprobates were converted here on a regular basis, he still missed the discipline and robed routine of the old church; saturated in phlegmatic devotion as the sublime chants of the choir emanated from above. He became nostalgic as he recalled the hallowed silence of the parishioners, as they awaited the tiny tinkling of bells, which seemed to orchestrate their service. These appeared to chase the heady perfume of incense down the cold stone-tiled aisles as the time-honoured organ drew the faithful to their knees. Its dulcet tones resonated round the massive marble columns, which themselves seemed rooted in time and tradition.

Another surprise this morning was the unswerving dogmatism of these proceedings. As everyone sang and clapped to the music, overhead projectors flooded the room, with words proclaiming,

"We share no shame; we share no blame
We have no fear; our God is here
In heaven He doth reign; it's clear
So ... all is right with the world."

Lee himself knew that, 'All is never … "right with the world",' for someone, somewhere, is being tortured, starved or raped. He raised this concept of unstinting faith with Tom, as they drove home, and queried the intense beliefs of these people.

Tom explained that this church was an evangelistic outreach, meaning they believed that everybody must repent and accept Jesus as Saviour, to be 'born again', and enter the kingdom of heaven. Lee had no desire to repent of anything, didn't believe in Jesus, or heaven and hell; and definitely didn't want to be born again, as he had had enough trouble first time around. So he listened in taciturn mode to what Tom was saying.

'These people are all fundamentalists, believing every word in the Bible,' he told Lee.

'What, even the bit about the talking snake, and the apple tree?' he asked.

'Yes, … the whole Garden of Eden thing. In fact, they believe all humanity stems from Adam and Eve, and is not just a parable!'

'But their version would involve incest, wouldn't it?' queried Lee.

'I suppose so, but they do take some bits more devoutly than others. For example, although Christ's first miracle was turning water into wine, they won't touch a drop of alcohol, even serving fruit juice at their Communion service. And many permit women to attend services without head-coverings, and to even preach on occasion, which the Bible clearly contradicts. They also subscribe to Tithing which is giving a tenth of your income to support the Pastors and maintain the church. That tradition is essential for churches to survive, but it arose in the Old Testament which relates how Abraham won a great battle and promised God a tenth of his income, if He would keep him safe in future battles, but the practise was later adopted as a form of tax to support the nation of Israel; but tithing is not mentioned in the New Testament, which speaks only of *gifting* whatever you feel you can afford.'

'At least they believe in Communion,' replied Lee.

'Well, ... kind of,' said Tom. 'They ignore Christ's declaration at the Last Supper that, ... "this is my body ... and this is my blood," preferring to believe that the bread and wine are mere symbols, or emblems.'

'But established churches like Catholics and Anglicans believe otherwise, - don't they?'

'I think so, Lee, but I'm no theologian, although I can tell you what I believe. Personally, I think all the different churches should either adhere to - or totally reject, this doctrine of *Transubstantiation*, as it's called, which is as fundamental a belief as the *Resurrection*, but enormous schism is generated because mainstream churches do subscribe to that belief; but it all revolves around faith.'

'What do you mean by faith,' queried Lee. 'What is it? I'm getting confused.'

'Well,' Tom replied. 'It's complicated, but without faith you cannot please God; but I should tell you, Lee, that compassion is by far the greatest virtue of all.'

'So, where do I find this faith? Is it inside the church?' puzzled Lee.

'No, it's everywhere; inside all of us, ready to awake! And faith can be found or lost, by any man, woman or child, usually in times of desperation,' Tom responded.

'Faith means never really understanding God's plan, but sensing that you understand perhaps a part of it; perhaps that part that is playing out in your own life. Faith is the evidence of things not seen, but just being confident of things you pray for, in the certainty that although you do not always see their immediate confirmation, your faith gives you title over the things you prayed for, as it hangs a conviction of belief that they will eventually mature.

Faith is what it means to have a soul and a spirit. But, to be wholly complete as a human being, you have to keep faith alive by exercising it like a muscle for the more you use it, the stronger it becomes. Adversity challenges you to do this, but if you neglect to exercise your faith, it may wither and die. There is nothing scientific or logical about it, but to gain from this gift of faith, you must deploy it. If you eventually lose your faith, it can only be your own fault, for an equal measure is granted to all.

It is best described as the unseen substance of hope. Like a bank-note, it promises the bearer a currency of goods, if used properly. I can see how anyone can lose faith by watching what goes on in the world; but just glancing at the heavens should inspire anyone ... to think twice.

We are mind, spirit, body and soul. Your soul is intrinsic to, but not the essence of your personality and until the advent of Cartesianism, most people, including all the great philosophers, believed all creatures had souls. Aristotle, possibly the greatest thinker in history, taught that wherever there is movement there is life, and where there is life there is soul. Two thousand years later the French Empiricist, Descartes – who concluded that proof of his own existence was simply the fact he could personally contemplate it - flew in the face of all classical philosophy by declaring that animals were mere automatons, ruled by instinct. He believed they were all soul-less entities, with hearts that were merely mechanical pumps; therefore, they could not experience emotions like pain. They only acted as if they did.

So, to prove his theory, he happily sliced dogs open and stuck his finger into their still-beating hearts; marvelling at how the valves opened and closed around his knuckle. He even practised on his wife's dog by nailing it spread-eagled to a wooden board and cutting it into pieces. He was totally un-fazed by the reactions of the dog or, apparently, his wife; perhaps because he believed that humans also possessed purely mechanical hearts, devoid of emotion. All we know now, is that the dog died shortly afterwards, in unimaginable agony. But, even today, vivisection scientists deploy Descartes' theories by claiming their objectors are merely engaging in "anthropomorphism", which is the attribution of personality to an animal, or thing. They claim that to believe animals possess personality is a gross error or even a sin! They also exercise this viewpoint to excuse their view of factory-farming, claiming its abuse and neglect of animals is totally logical and rational in a modern age.

But the new discipline of neuro-cardiology proves that the heart is a sensory organ, which can receive and process information. Apparently, it has an extensive neural network linking it to the brain, and throughout the body, to which it communicates via electromagnetic field interactions.

'You're losing me,' said Lee, 'this is all too complicated; just slow down!'

'Okay,' Tom said patiently. 'The nervous system within the "heart-brain" enables it to learn, remember and function, *independent* of the brain's cerebral cortex, which it can even influence regarding perception, cognition and emotion. It is now assumed that people can actually die from the emotion of "heart-break", and if you try to subdue your "heart-felt" emotions you eventually become "heart-less." Indeed … if you have a heart transplant, you may develop feelings and sympathies, which the actual donor possessed. I have just read the latest case-histories in a recent Nexus magazine, where many such cases were clinically documented.'

'Really! … Do tell,' said Lee, cynically.

'Well, there is one study, where a twenty-four-year-old artist was on her way to open her first art exhibition at a lesbian bookstore when a drunk driver ploughed into her. She was a very sensual gay lady, and her heart was donated to a twenty-five-year-old male graduate. He now feels he has a woman's way of thinking; even about sex. His girlfriend now claims he mostly wants to cuddle and hold her all the time. He now loves shopping, even carrying a purse, which he slings over his shoulder.'

'That's just an anomaly,' declared Lee.

'Not really,' stated Tom. 'There are lots of similar phenomena, recorded worldwide.'

'Tell me more,' said Lee, intrigued.

'Well, Doctor Paul Pearsall PhD. has chronicled over seventy case-histories, including the story of a seventeen-year-old black male, who was shot dead in a drive-by shooting, while on his way to violin class. He died in the street, hugging his violin case. His recipient was a forty-seven-year-old foundry worker whose wife states he frequently brings his black work colleagues home now - which he never did before. She also reports that he drives her nuts with classical music, which he listens to for hours, whistling songs he has never heard before. She is quoted, as saying, - "You'd think he might be into rap-music, having the heart of a black man!".'

'That's funny,' said Lee.

'Maybe, but many serious issues arise from heart transplants! Like the case of an eighteen-year-old boy, whose father is a renowned psychiatrist. This boy, who died in a car accident, was a very talented musician, writing poetry and songs, one of which was titled, "Danni, my heart is yours." His heart was transplanted into an eighteen-year-old girl. Her father claims she was once a bit of a hell-raiser, who never liked musical instruments, but now loves to play the guitar, which was her donor's prime love. Her name, by the way, is Danni.'

'That is so sad,' said Lee, tearfully.

'Well, we were talking about animals, so let me tell you about a nineteen-year-old woman, called Sara, who ran a health-food restaurant. She was into free-love and had many different lovers, but was killed when a car slammed into her. Her recipient, called Susie, claims she was the 'queen' of the Big-Mac and was MacDonald's biggest customer. She claims she was gay before the operation, but now women don't turn her on at all. In fact, … she is currently engaged to be married to a young man. She also says the smell of meat makes her throw up, and won't have it in the house because when she smells it she sometimes feels the intense impact of the car, which slammed into her donor!'

'That is absolutely amazing,' Lee concluded. 'I'm stunned.'

'Let me give you one more example,' said Tom. 'This case involves the killing of a thirty-four-year-old police officer, called Carl. He was shot in the face, at point-blank range, as he attempted to arrest a drug dealer. His recipient was a fifty-six-year-old college professor. He initially claimed his main reaction after the surgery were flashes of bright light and an intense burning sensation in his face. He told his wife about the flashes of light, which he experiences at odd times of the day and night. He also told her, but *not* his doctors, of the many glimpses of Jesus, which always seem to accompany these flashbacks.'

'And this guy is a college professor! Don't tell me anymore,' said Lee, in shock. 'It's just too much; I can't handle it.'

'Well ... Okay! Let's just say it now seems obvious that Descartes was wrong, and Aristotle was right.'

When he dropped Lee off at the flats, Tom agreed to call round the next day. When he arrived the next morning, he found Lee in a buoyant mood.

Over tea and toast, Lee informed him that the computer class, which he attended, had helped his reading and writing. He had acquired basic keyboard skills, so now intended to purchase a decent computer and get on the internet, to educate himself. Tom became alarmed for he knew Lee was a recent victim of unrequited love, and was in a lonely place, emotionally.

'I must warn you Lee, about the internet, for I was a counsellor, for people addicted to things on the Web.'

'Do you mean games and gambling?' said Lee, aware that Tom knew most Chinese people loved gambling, and that it was a powerful addiction.

'No, I'm afraid not. I'm talking here about pornography and how you can get addicted to that, just like a drug. Do you have any idea of what's out there, waiting for you?'

Lee told him about the old man in the park, who had warned him about certain things.

Tom spoke, 'There are many other things that you don't know about, which I think I should tell you. When we held counselling sessions, we realised that all sorts of people had all sorts of weaknesses for all sorts of fetishes, and nobody seemed immune. We had barristers, architects, judges, police-officers, even church pastors and doctors who joined our group sessions, because they sensed some habits were getting beyond their conscious control. The irony is that most were married and loved their wives, but felt unfulfilled, and anxious to try out new things while they were still capable.

I even know of people who claim the internet is a form of Antichrist; a toolbox of the Devil, and they avoid all contact with it. It is interesting to reflect it was first invented by the military as a tool of war. Many people consider that mankind has a penchant for self-destruction and self-harm, and that's what I think you need to be aware of, Lee!'

'So,' queried Lee, 'what exactly should I look out for?'

'Well, there are a multitude of websites out there, catering to an enormous variety of fetishes, from mere peccadillos to the most outrageous abominations. They bizarrely entice the voyeur, perhaps latent in us all to identify and relate to characters of extreme beauty, reacting in extreme fashion to extreme circumstance. The players tend to represent lost opportunities for the viewer who feels they may have missed out on some of life's experiences and so become surrogates for them, in that respect!'

'I have seen adverts, on television, for an amazing variety of sex toys,' Lee responded.

'Perhaps, ... but it's not all fun and games. There are literally tens of thousands of 'phone-call' sites where women will, for five pounds a minute, humour any of your fantasies no matter how weird and wonderful they may be.'

'But just how strange can they be?' asked Lee.

'I will just mention a few aberrations which people get drawn into, through a lust for power and control. For example, there are sites where voluptuous women expose themselves to men who feel the need to be dominated. Not just physically, but financially as well.'

'What! You mean the women entice men to give them money … for nothing?'

'Yes,' replied Tom. 'The men may feel guilty about having too much, and this is exploited by ruthless women on a regular basis, who advertise for money slaves.'

'Unbelievable,' commented Lee.

'No, Lee; what really is unbelievable are the elaborate degrees to which people, mostly men, will go to be punished and humiliated. In fact, a professional dominatrix may delight in the pain she can inflict, without consequence, and of course the money she may receive for her services,' said Tom.

'I can think of better ways of spending my money,' said Lee.

'Let's hope it stays like that, my friend,' said Tom, as he dropped Lee off at the block of flats.

Lee awoke, after a night plagued by nightmares. He had dreams he wanted to forget, which he did, after a few coffees. He plodded his way to the park, and met up with Lucy, whom he now learned was the leader of the animal rights activists. A discussion arose when Lee ordered his breakfast of bacon, egg and sausage. Some of the group got up to leave, showing distaste for this carnivore, but settled down again to argue their case with Lee who pleaded ignorance to their beliefs.

'Don't you know what sausages are made from?' asked Lucy.

'Of course … meat,' he answered.

'Yes, but what sort of meat?' she queried.

'Pork and beef, mostly,' Lee replied.

'Well actually, it's mostly mechanically recovered meat, known as MRM, which is stripped from the bones of dead cows.'

'Wow,' he replied, 'I never knew that.'

Lucy continued. 'Did you know that when the sausage meat is blasted off the carcass by high-pressure hoses, it is gathered up and pumped through the animals' hollow intestines, to encase it like a condom? In fact, some condom manufacturers now use animal intestines as condom sheaths, for they claim it provides a more "natural" feeling.'

Lee now found he was starting to sympathise with the group's motives for he too, had become an animal lover. Nevertheless, he decided to question their ethics, regarding his choice of breakfast.

'Eating animals is natural,' he said. 'We have been doing it since prehistoric times. We need to eat meat to be strong and healthy.'

'No, we don't,' said Lucy, 'for the strongest animals on Earth are the gorillas, and they don't eat meat.'

'But mankind has been eating meat for thousands of years,' Lee objected.

She continued. 'We are the most highly evolved mammals and were designed to eat the highest evolved foods. Our ancient ancestors were all frugivores, living mostly on fruit, and only started to hunt out of necessity.'

'Okay, countered Lee, 'but both man and animals have evolved since then, and will continue to evolve, and if you lived in a place like China, or a remote jungle, killing animals for food and clothes could be considered justified.'

'Only in a primitive environment,' Lucy responded, 'but certainly not civilised, for herding thirty-thousand chickens into a concrete warehouse all their lives, where they never see daylight or scratch in soil can never be justified.'

'I'm still not convinced. Give me a few facts?' asked Lee.

Lucy explained. 'Well, animals in a slaughterhouse sense when they are due for slaughter. For example, they smell the adrenalin of intense fear, in others around them.

So their meat is full of cholesterol, adrenalin and toxins when they are killed. Do you not realise that mammals, which eat meat like big cats, lap water up with their tongue whereas vegetarian species, like gorillas, or giraffes simply suck water like humans do? That alone implies we should be vegetarian, and avoid meat, which is at the bottom of the food chain.'

'It's not at the bottom of my food chain,' said Lee. 'My canine teeth would fall out if I stopped eating meat. That's what they were designed for.'

Lucy responded. 'With the exception of rodents and rabbits, all mammals have canine teeth, and several herbivores have ferocious canine teeth, a prime example being the animal that kills more humans than all other wildlife in Africa, the hippopotamus. It possesses canine teeth over a foot long, but even some forest deer have long protruding canine teeth.'

'Thanks for reminding me,' joked Lee, 'got to have one of mine filled next week!'

'I must tell you, Lee,' said Lucy, 'that my dentist told me recently that he had to treat a patient who later revealed, after treatment, that he had developed the CJD prion, from a BSE infection, which people caught from eating hamburgers. My dentist told me he had to dispose of every surgical instrument in his surgery, because even autoclaving cannot sterilize stainless steel instruments after contact with this infection because it requires temperatures of over a thousand degrees Fahrenheit, and autoclaves only heat up to two hundred and fifty degrees.'

Lucy's friends were then joined by a small group of 'sabbers', which Lee discovered was slang for 'hunt saboteurs.' He heard they had been out the previous day sabbing a hunt. They had set false trails for the huntsmen, putting the hounds off the scent of the fox.

But when the hunt caught up with them they lashed out with their riding crops and drove their horses into the group, while the local police did nothing but video the proceedings. Apparently, the police needed records and profiles for their database, so the sabbers wore scarfs and balaclavas to hide their identity. Lee learned that when bystanders tried to fend off hordes of hounds with garden rakes, the master of the Surrey Union Hunt, at the time, one Rosemary Peters, idly stood by with her entourage as her hounds ripped a cornered stag to pieces; but new laws caused the Heythrop Hunt, which former Prime Minister Cameron rode with, to be prosecuted by the RSPCA for illegal hunting and fined over twenty-six-thousand pounds.

Another of the group spoke up. 'Meat eaters perspire through their tongues and have claws, whereas humans only perspire through their skin. Also meat eaters have acid saliva, which contains no enzymes to digest grains, but human saliva is alkaline, with ptyalin enzymes for digesting grains. Humans also possess molars with which to grind grains, whereas meat eaters have no molars. Besides, our intestinal systems are much more complicated than animals, for carnivores like lions have a big intestine of only a few feet, unlike ours. Even our small intestine is over twenty-foot long and much more sophisticated, so meat which takes a long time to filter through the human system, creating toxins, is excreted in hours by meat-eating animals. However, a huge factor now in our modern diet is the amount of gluten and sugar in common everyday foods.'

'What do you mean?' queried Lee.

'Well,' she explained, 'since nineteen-twenty-five many eminent scientists have fervently believed that not only is sugar directly related to diabetes and obesity, but that all human cancers could be starved to death, by totally eliminating the intake of sugar, which is essential to their survival. They claim that all cancer cells need to ferment glucose to sustain and survive. And in regards to gluten, mankind has eaten wheat, a hybrid of three grasses, for ten thousand years but in the late sixties the big wheat growers massively raised the ordinary gluten content of wheat to increase production and profit. Gluten is described as the perfect human poison but is pumped into almost all processed foods, from soup to sweets. It is fractionalized from wheat-flour by washing the starch granules out of the dough, but when used in mass production, is added as a powder to dough in massive amounts. The actual genome of wheat consists of over twenty-three thousand different proteins, having five times the DNA of the human body and even contains seventeen thousand-million base-pairs; but gluten itself is a protein. It is used to trap air and gas in bread to make it rise quickly. Bread is our main staple food but unfortunately gluten is now a chronic toxin for humans, as it cannot be completely broken down in human guts.'

Lucy intervened, 'I read recently that the 'gluten-free' market in the States alone is worth more than five billion dollars a year, because thirty-per-cent of the population now strive for a gluten-free diet. Only one-per-cent of them are Celiacs, but the rest find their general health vastly improves, alleviating headaches, wind, joint pain and even epilepsy, but unfortunately, worldwide gluten consumption has tripled in the last few decades.'

She continued. 'The fact is ... we would all live a lot longer if we ate fresh foods, instead of dead flesh, but the food industry will only push the most profitable cheapest items, regardless of the methods used to furnish them.

Let's face it; the food industry is responsible for over half the world's organic water pollution. But not only is this being aggravated by things like fracking, the very earth is contaminated, and even the air we breathe is now toxic, for in some countries people have to walk around with masks over their mouths. In fact, nearly half our current population will be afflicted by some form of cancer in their lifetime.'

Lee was stunned. 'That's staggering,' he exclaimed. 'Unbelievable!'

Lucy then told him, 'Apparently, the U.K. food and farming industry has an annual turnover of more than a hundred-thousand-million pounds but is increasingly aware of public concern regarding the use of fertilisers, pesticides and antibiotics.

Unfortunately, the industry currently chooses to ignore the massively detrimental effect on either the consumer or the environment. We now know that diet is the main reason why a quarter of young men have very low sperm counts; although half the pregnancies that do occur, are not planned. In fact, modern processed foods use so many preservatives, colours, sweeteners, stabilisers, flavour-enhancers and emulsifiers that you need a magnifying glass to read the long list of additives.'

'Is that because there are so many additives now, that they have trouble listing them all on the label?' queried someone.

'Partly, I suppose, but they don't really want you to see what they have corrupted your food with. Years ago the big companies listed all those ingredients as

"E" numbers. Then lots of booklets were printed listing exactly what these stood for, and everyone discovered the lower the number, the more toxic the additive. The firms then reverted to long, complicated chemical names and shoppers now have little, or no idea, what they're buying.'

Lee spoke up. 'What about calcium loss; we need milk to build up our bones, don't we?' he suggested.

'That's rubbish,' stated one of the sabbers. 'The milk myth is a cultural phenomenon, which can be traced back thousands of years, but modern research proves that not only do we barely absorb any calcium in pasteurised milk, but that milk actually increases calcium loss from our bones. This is because all animal protein acidifies the PH levels in the human body. This then triggers a biological reaction, because calcium is the perfect acid-neutraliser, and we store most of our calcium in our bones, which is then taken to neutralise the acidifying effect of milk. Once calcium is pulled out of the bones it leaves via the urine so the net result is an actual calcium deficit. Current statistics prove that countries with the lowest consumption of dairy products have the lowest fracture incidence in their populations. Most ailments like acid reflux, arthritis, and diabetes are linked to diet. Perhaps due to ancient survival needs we adapted to drinking other species' milk, but in other mammals, once their calves are weaned they never drink milk again. Having said that, we should bear in mind that a human mother's milk is excellent nutrition for babies, but its composition is completely different to cow's milk.'

Lee declared, 'People with weak bones are always advised to drink more milk.'

Lucy then stated, 'A twelve-year Harvard study found those people who consumed the most calcium from dairy foods broke more bones than those who rarely drank milk. The human body triggers a protective reaction to neutralise the damaging acidic protein of milk before it reaches the kidneys and the urinary tract. The body then leaches calcium from the bones as the most readily available source of acid neutraliser, so even though milk contains calcium, it ends up sapping your bones of that crucial mineral.'

She carried on. 'Raw milk is far less acidic than consumer milk, which is now pasteurised by law and homogenised, causing a long list of digestive and cancer-inducing catalysts. This is because dairy cows are given antibiotics and injected with genetically engineered bovine-growth hormones to artificially increase milk production. Unfortunately, this increases the levels of an insulin growth factor, "IGF-1", in all humans who drink milk and higher levels of that factor are conclusively linked to several human cancers.'

Someone interrupted Lucy. 'Did you know that the U.N. recently declared that the livestock sector, which incidentally hosts one and a half billion cows, generates eighteen-per-cent more greenhouse gas than all the emissions from all the transport around the world. Most analysts agree that eighty-per-cent of all antibiotics produced by the pharmaceutical companies are used in animal farming. It's worth noting that the pharmaceutical

cancers would die out. At the moment most crops are grown in depleted soil, and even basic essential elements, like Iodine, are taken out of ordinary salt. However, no government could sustain a populace where most of its citizens lived to be a hundred, so they all have a vested interest in maintaining the status-quo, for if people lived much longer governments would need to spread some lethal pandemic virus, probably through genetically mutated mosquitos, to curb our population growth.'

One of the sabbers then stated. 'Did you know that dogs and even people can be cloned genetically to produce perfect replicas of themselves?'

'I find that hard to believe,' claimed Lee.

'Well, I can tell you,' she replied, 'there is an American institute called "Genetic-Savings and Clone", which is a commercial gene-bank, prepared to clone almost anything, but they charge fifty thousand pounds for just cloning a cat, so it's not a viable option for most grieving owners.'

Lee felt queasy over all these revelations so, on leaving the group, went straight home to bed without even eating.

CHAPTER NINE

The following morning Lee felt much better and ventured forth for a bite to eat in the café. Lucy was there with the others so he bought them all some coffees, as he ordered his breakfast.

'Did you know,' Lucy told him, 'that in recent times, manufacturers like Coke-Cola paid to have a subliminal image of their product periodically flashed across the theatre screen, while the public were watching a movie. When the interval arose loads of people would rush to buy the drink in question, although none had consciously seen anything on the screen, except the actual movie.'

'That would have been a science-fiction movie, then?' laughed Lee.

'Well, the government actually had to ban that practice, but you do realise that fact is stranger than fiction, so watch out in future and enjoy your hamburger,' said Lucy.

'And my bacon, egg and sausage,' retorted Lee.

'Don't you remember, Lee,' someone else pointed out, 'that back in two-thousand and fifteen the World Health Organisation publically stated bacon and sausages were proved to provoke cancers in humans?'

'Okay,' agreed Lee, 'everyone accepts the cancer risk in meat and cigarettes, but all things in moderation is the sensible approach.'

'Well, I don't think it's sensible to get a moderate dose of cancer, do you Lee?' asked Lucy.

'And,' she added, 'don't you realise we shouldn't kill an animal for any reason, other than saving a human life? We live in a civilised environment now, with many food alternatives, so we don't need to eat meat or wear fur, therefore we shouldn't kill animals for that purpose.'

'But we save lives by experimenting on animals, and they wouldn't even be born if we didn't breed them for research, which is a legitimate reason to kill them,' said Lee.

Lucy responded, 'That's crazy. It's like saying that if you bred babies in a dark dungeon all their lives, only to kill them when they grew to maturity, they would still be better off than if they were never born, in the first place!

Let me tell you, that in twenty-fourteen in Northern Ireland, researchers in the two big universities there slaughtered twenty-thousand animals including dogs, cats and sheep. The researchers themselves admitted that at least a thousand of the animals were subjected to severe suffering. In one study mice were fed a high-fat diet for five months until they became obese. Then a drug called Sitagliptin was force-fed via a tube down their throats for three weeks. They were subjected to repeated blood-sampling and injections straight into their stomachs. At the end of the study they were pickled alive, to have their brains removed. Rodents were also force-fed pure lavender oil, after being tortured with bright lights and extreme noise levels, to stress them out.

They are not alone because an organisation, the Union for the Abolition of Vivesection, recently revealed that in the Porton-Down Laboratories in Wiltshire, government scientists carried out cruel and grotesque research where guinea pigs were poisoned to death. Also, marmosets were given Anthrax and Bubonic plague in germ warfare experiments. Military surgeons shot healthy pigs and even strapped them down to blow them up with bombs - placed less than ten feet away, in order to gauge the effectiveness of new ordinance and the variety of wounds it would inflict. A government spokesman stated, "We are very proud of the work that we do here!"

It makes me burn with shame in having to share this world with those who sacrifice the sanctity of life on the altar of industry. The right to life is equal for all, animals and humans alike, as they are individually created by God for a purpose, whether you do, or do not, understand His intentions. This means that we cannot justify medical experiments that involve killing animals, usually slowly and painfully, by the number of human lives that particular experiment may save.'

'Well, I'm afraid I don't believe in your God,' retorted Lee.

'Okay,' Lucy replied, 'so let's look at it logically then! Any act is wrong if it produces more suffering than it alleviates. If someone or something has the gift of life they will possess desires, emotions, perception, memory, and the ability to react to circumstance. In other words, they are sentient, which is the common capacity all life shares.'

'But,' said Lee, 'animals cannot discern rationally, the way we do, so don't possess the same equal rights as us.'

Lucy replied. 'Surely animals have the right to live their lives free from suffering and exploitation? In regards to equality the question is not can they reason, or talk, but can they suffer, and all animals have the ability to suffer in a similar way human beings do. All creatures have the ability to not only feel pain and pleasure, but also fear, loneliness and motherly love. Are you telling me a fly won't mind if you tear its wing off, or a fish won't react if you stick a pin in it? Or that crabs and lobsters relish being boiled alive? Every animal values its own life and fights for survival, as do humans.'

'Maybe,' Lee agreed, 'but fish and invertebrates are cold blooded, so feel no pain.'

'Well,' said Lucy, 'don't be so sure. Fish have very sophisticated nervous systems, especially in the fins and gills, and scientists who cut the tail-fins off tropical Zebra fish did another 'Pavlov' test where they starved them, along with a group of 'control' zebras, which nobody had experimented on before. They had initially introduced the finless fish into a tank dosed with an analgesic, in the form of aspirin, which helped them settle down. When their fins grew back the same fish had the same fins removed again, before being put together with the healthy control fish, into a different tank, where two compartments were available for any of the fish to enter. The normal hungry fish all swam into a warm heated section with bright lighting and lots of food, but the damaged fish entered a cold hostile environment where there was no food, or light.'

'So fish are dumb,' Lee concluded.

'Not exactly,' said Lucy. 'The hostile environment contained an aspirin solution in the water, so those fish made a rational decision to ignore their hunger, and alleviate the more severe pain of mutilation. This proves they were not only aware of their pain, but were also susceptible to subjective states because their memory told them they could benefit from certain actions. So we should now classify fish as sentient entities.'

'Well, what about invertebrates … they are at the bottom of the food chain, aren't they?' queried Lee.

'Sorry, Lee, can't agree with you on that one either,' said Lucy. 'In zoos, keepers have found that different breeds of octopus could solve puzzles faster than the people who invented those puzzles.'

She continued. 'Some people emphatically assert that an animal's life is only valuable because of the happiness it contains and distributes, so if they kill it, but rear another in its place, they have not reduced the degree of happiness in the world. However, we know that animals bred for factory farming are certainly not happy, and are normally not slaughtered painlessly.'

'But we will still need to kill them, in experiments, to save human lives,' insisted Lee.

'Why? It's illegal to kill babies for food or experiments, yet they are no different in their psychological capacities than animals,' continued Lucy.

'But babies develop and grow into rational entities,' Lee insisted.

'Babies are mostly irrational, as are some adults with mental disabilities, so if we cannot differentiate their psychological capacities from those of animals, then to deny any animal a right to life on those grounds cannot be justified. Furthermore, animals, like humans, develop an identity over time and construct patterns for routines in their lives, which matter greatly to them.'

'What!' Lee retorted, 'are you telling me animals are equal to humans?'

'Well, all mammals mature and develop identity, and sentience. In fact, the religion of Buddhism, which is the fourth largest in the world with five-hundred-million followers, preaches that every living creature on Earth is sacred and must be respected.'

'But,' said Lee, 'all animals do not have the same right to life, as a human being does.'

'Why not?' Lucy asked. 'Regarding survival, our society does not discriminate between "more valuable" and "less valuable" human beings, so we should not discriminate between more valuable and less valuable animals. Even insects and flies are essential in maintaining the status-quo of life.'

'How come?' queried Lee.

'Well, flies are consumed by spiders and if not for them we would be knee deep in flies, who devour waste and mess, but spiders in turn feed the birds. And if bees ceased to exist very little would get pollinated and crops would fail, and eventually the human race would simply die out, for bees underpin the sustenance of life. But the bee population is in trouble now, with mites and pollution, in the form of pesticides.'

'In what respect?' queried somebody.

Lucy explained. 'Many bees are getting addicted to widely-used chemical pesticides, three forms of which have been banned by the E.U. These are called neo-nicotinoids and contribute to a decline in bees, because they get addicted to the nicotine-sprayed nectar, in the same way that humans get addicted to cigarettes. And when bee-keepers winter their hives they often use a swarm-catching pheromone to lure bees into greenhouses, where they are fed refined white sugar, supplemented on occasion by pollen substitutes. Needless to say, their natural life-span is reduced by years, for they should be allowed to eat their own honey to survive; but this method enables some unscrupulous breeders to harvest that honey, as a matter of economics. Also, when they mix that sugar with specific amounts of water, the keepers are able to encourage certain behaviour patterns in those greenhouse bees.'

One of the sabbers then stated. 'As you know, bees not only pollinate; they make honey, but ninety-per-cent of honey in the shops is actually fake honey.'

'What on earth do you mean by that?' said Lee, confused.

'Well, Chinese medical researchers discovered, decades ago, the incredible benefits of bee-pollen in regards to allergies, viral-immunity and longevity. Being experts at mass manufacturing and imitation, they produced a very cheap type of honey for export, containing pollen substitutes mixed with contaminants, such as chloramphenicol, which is a common antibiotic. They exported many tons of this low-grade honey around the world, principally to the United States, who then tested its DNA, suspecting it was corrupted. Discovering its Chinese origin, the U.S. immediately banned its importation. They then sent it back to China, where it was then mixed with pollen and viola-plant extracts, to legalise it.

The Chinese later developed the process of Ultra-Filtration, which removed all the pollen from the honey, for their own needs. They also gave it a very long shelf-life by sweetening it with high-fructose-corn-syrup, or HFCS, but this is linked to diabetes, obesity, liver damage and plaque build-up, but this process is now used world-wide, so now the vast majority of 'supermarket' honey is only useful as a sweetener, and nutritionally useless, having now evolved into an actual health risk.'

Lee was then asked to join the movement, who now felt that he resonated with their beliefs. On reflection, he decided to distance himself, for he knew that undercover police often infiltrated such anarchic groups and he now needed to keep a low profile.

He listened to the group, planning a trip to Dover the following weekend to protest against horses being delivered to the Continent for meat in restaurants. He heard the truck drivers involved were totally indifferent to the plight of the horses in their care, because they realised the beasts would soon be slaughtered.

Apparently, they never bother to feed or water the starving animals, and when faced with protesters, which often include elderly folks, the long-distance truck-drivers throw their bottles of urine, collected on the journey, all over the protesters.

Lucy added. 'Thank God we are leaving the E.U., because their animal abuse is far worse than in England. Tens of thousands of cattle from Europe are frequently exported to cheap backward abattoirs in Morocco, where brutal and medieval methods of slaughter are deployed. The exhausted, dehydrated animals that have travelled thousands of miles in double-decker trucks without food, water or shade are permanently tethered with their legs shackled, so have to be dragged out as these trucks have no ramps.'

As Lee listened to various tales from around the country, including the way young badgers were gassed by farmers, he got very indignant.

'Surely farmers love animals, and would tend to any animals and livestock on their land,' he declared.

This remark was greeted with a chorus of derision.

'Farmers don't love animals. They are merely chattels to generate income.'

'So tell me,' queried Lee, 'where did all that mad-cow disease come from?'

'Well,' said Lucy, 'that originated because of farmers feeding the remains of dead cattle, in a mix of bone-meal, to their own cows, who are strict herbivores and shouldn't even eat meat. Even today, cows are fed un-natural diets to maximise growth and milk output, which is constant, for dairy cows must be kept pregnant to keep their milk flowing. They are confined indoors in winter, and sometimes even all year round, and may never, in their whole lives, see the sky or even a blade of grass; and they are constantly bloated and in pain. Most are genetically manipulated with the dairy-cow hormone, BGH, to make them produce ten times more milk than their calves actually need. Because of this abuse they develop painful mastitis to their teats, which produce pus, and this pus sometimes ends up in the milk. Antibiotics have then to be painfully injected into the cow, through the teat itself, to treat this potentially fatal infection.

When they reach the end of their useful lives as dairy cows they are taken to be cruelly slaughtered with inefficient stun-guns, ending up as hamburgers on your plate, most of which contain bone, gristle and fat. Burgers on their own, contain on average, only about twelve per cent actual meat, which itself is stained red by "lipid colouring", usually chlorophyll or melanin, and the average burger is fifty per-cent moisture and up to thirty per-cent fat. In fact, any hamburger aficionado will tell you the cheapest burgers are the tastiest, whereas a real-meat burger doesn't taste half as nourishing, for a lot of tasty additives are left out.'

Somebody commented, 'Look how they rear pigs by imprisoning the sow on her side in a cage, where she cannot move, so the baby piglets can have milk all the time. And tell me,' she added, 'do you have any idea how little time a new-born lamb remains with its mother, before being dragged off to be slaughtered, leaving that mother sheep bleating for days on end?'

Lucy joined in, 'Lee, do you know anything at all about factory farming?' she asked.

'Not a lot ... except it keeps the price of food down,' he said with confidence.

'Yes, ... but what price do we pay in the end?' she asked him. 'Did you know that even fish now have their genomes altered, for profit? The Federal Drug Administration has just licensed a fish farm in Panama to produce genetically altered fish eggs, which grow to maturity in half the time. At the moment they only breed super-salmon with these, but plans are in place to genetically modify another fifty species; and if any of those escape into the oceans they could breed with wild varieties to potentially wipe out the whole species. Anyway, you should only eat fish from rivers or lakes because most ocean varieties are contaminated with mercury from worldwide pollution. Apart from herrings whose skin seems immune to mercury absorption, most ocean fish, especially mackerel, swordfish, and shark should be shunned by pregnant mothers and children to avoid mercury poisoning.'

'How on earth, or should I say, ... sea - can mercury end up in the ocean?' queried Lee.

'Well,' she replied, 'most of it comes from human activities, like burning fossil-fuels, especially coal. Every year the United States alone release hundreds of tonnes of mercury into the air, where rainfall washes it into the rivers and oceans; but industrial complexes around the world constantly discharge mercury-laden effluents into rivers. This alone would not pose a health risk if the mercury was not converted by the oceans into methyl-mercury, which diffuses into plankton and so passes up the food-chain. Now predator fish, such as tuna, contain ten-million times the amount of methyl-mercury as the water surrounding them. Because heavy-metal poisons are depleted through organs like lungs and kidneys, and the skin is the biggest human organ, mercury poisoning can sometimes render your skin a nice zombie-like shade of graveyard-grey!'

Lee then asked if it was the mercury that was driving whales onto beaches around the world.

Lucy told him. 'Nobody knows, but those whales are just a *drop in the ocean*, if you'll pardon the pun, Lee. Whales are killed mostly for blubber, which is used by cosmetics firms for everything from glossy lipsticks and perfume right down to ordinary soap.

Unfortunately, the Japanese government still sanctions whaling; they disingenuously claim it is necessary for their medical research, but Lee, I must tell you … whales are also killed for sport.'

'I don't believe you,' Lee protested. 'Nobody would kill a whale for sport!' he cried.

'Well, Denmark, an anti-whaling member of the E.U., and subject to laws prohibiting the slaughter of all cetaceans, collaborates with the Faroe-Islanders, when they hold their annual "Grindadrap". Hundreds of whales are driven by fishing vessels under the auspices of the Danish navy, onto the beaches, where thousands of local islanders gleefully run into the water to cut and slice the whales to pieces; the very sea turns red: blood-red.'

'So the whales aren't the only animals on the beach, then?' Lee wryly commented.

'Please don't class those butchers in the same category as some of nature's most noble specimens,' said Lucy, 'but let me tell you, whales aren't the only animals killed for sport.'

'Really … just people, out hunting. - Right?' queried Lee.

'Um … no, Lee. In bull-rings and fiestas around the world, a quarter of a million healthy bulls are butchered every year, for legal and illegal entertainment.'

'But that's just a cultural thing, which has prospered for centuries,' Lee exclaimed.

'Culture is no excuse for cruelty,' replied Lucy.

'The matadors will only fight a weakened bull, so before these bulls are released into the ring, they are horrendously abused before the events. They have wet newspapers stuffed into their ears and cotton pushed up their nostrils, to limit their breathing. Petroleum jelly is then rubbed into their eyes to blur their vision, and their genitals are pierced with needles, to enrage them. They often have their horns shaved to put them off-balance and, to prevent them lying down in the ring, strong caustic solutions are rubbed on their legs. Just before they are prodded into the ring with daggers, a rosette is stapled onto their neck as a target for the matador, pointing out the exact spot where the neck nerves are most vulnerable!' Observing Lee's shocked reaction, Lucy elaborated.

'After four flowery darts are placed in its spine, during the first "faenas", or passes, heralded by choruses of "ole's", the bull will then be unable to raise its head properly, ... but may still present a hazard to the matador. The banderillos, or flagmen, will now pierce its back muscles with more harpoon-like barbed spears! If the bull is still feisty after this, the picadors, mounted on blinkered armoured horses corner the wounded beast, jabbing their long lances into it; then the brave matador recuperates to deliver the coup-de-grace with a long sword to the heart. This action is supposed to take just one thrust, but always takes more! The ears are then cut off, and presented by the matador to his favoured senorita in the crowd. The victim is then towed away to be skinned, and even then, may still be conscious. If by some miracle, or botch-up, a resilient bull is left standing, the crowd may yell for an Indulto, or pardon, for the condemned creature. In the Plaza bull ring in Mexico City, which hosts fifty thousand spectators, an Indulto was granted to a bull, which survived to sire a hundred calves. Its owner, Senor Hose Fernandez, then took it to Canada to get it cloned; so matadors - beware!'

'Damn … I never realised it was such a cruel blood-sport.' Lee responded.

'Well … yes, but I wonder, Lee,' said Lucy, 'if you happen to know about the way fur-seals are butchered around the world?' she asked.

'I remember reading that in the backwards African country of Namibia, a hundred thousand fur-seals are cruelly slaughtered every year, by men with metal-hooked clubs.' Lee responded.

'Ah, yes, but what about Canada, which is not a third-world country, even claiming to be civilised?'

'Don't tell me! What do they get up to?' cried Lee.

'Since 1966, the Canadian government has poured millions of dollars a year into subsidising the commercial seal slaughter, and fur-marketing of baby harp-seals. The hunters callously chase and club baby seals to death with ice-picks, year after year. The Canadian government issued quotas in twenty-fifteen for half-a-million kills.'

'Seems that innocent animals get a raw deal on this planet,' Lee concluded.

'Yes,' Lucy agreed, 'but let me tell you that in Pakistan the sport of bear-baiting is prevalent, which involves chaining young bears by the nose, to metal stakes - so large fighting dogs can attack them. The bears have their teeth and claws pulled, so cannot defend themselves, and that torture goes on for hours.'

'Well … it doesn't surprise me in a country like that.' said Lee.

'Okay … but it's also very popular in the United States; and so is 'penning', where foxes are penned up in compounds to be set upon by vicious dogs who rip them to shreds!'

'I'm beginning to believe in the Devil, if not God,' Lee declared. 'Man seems to be the vilest beast on this planet,' he concluded.

'I agree,' said Lucy, 'but genetically modified foods may destroy all of us before long, if we're not careful,' said Lucy.

'What makes you say that?' said Lee, astounded.

'Surely genetically modified foods produce much more yield than conventional crops, and were designed to feed the starving masses around the world.'

'The road to hell is paved with good intentions,' Lucy replied, 'and the Devil is called Monsanto. This giant independent corporation became infamous after producing DDT, Dioxin and Agent Orange; it also invented the cancer-inducing sweeteners, Aspartame and Saccharin.

This firm has become notorious for its efforts in the mass production of genetically modified seeds, which were designed to be fertile for one season only. This means farmers cannot save or re-plant any seeds, so are forced to purchase new seed stock year after year, from Monsanto, of course. These are called "terminator" seeds. They also manufacture "Roundup", the most toxic, best-selling pesticide on planet-earth. They even supply synthetic growth hormones, like BGH, for large animal feeding operations. But whether through meat or dairy consumption this hormone-induced imbalance contributes to cancerous tumour formations in humans who consume their products.

By nineteen-ninety-six Monsanto were able to control transgenic varieties of soybean and peanuts, amongst other crops, and by two-thousand and five had evolved into the world's most powerful controller of GM foods and seeds. They spend many millions on governmental lobbying, even infiltrating the Clinton and Obama legislatures, and still frequently defeat moves by public protest groups, who demand that these modified foods, quaintly known as "Franken-foods", should be labelled as genetically-modified in stores and shops around the world. But they are not alone for an Oakland based firm, DNA Plant Technology, put the anti-freeze gene from a flounder-fish into a tomato, which became known as one of the "Flavr-Savr" brands. This extends its shelf-life to forty-five days and makes it resistant to frost conditions, and was even approved by the F.D.A., before public outrage banned it.'

'So, that idea floundered, then,' cried Lee, bemused.

'You could say that, but it's no joking matter,' said Lucy, 'for before the advent of factory farming and genetically modified foods mankind led a relatively un-polluted life; but we are what we eat, so corrupted foods breed corrupted bodies and corrupted brains.'

'How could your brain possibly get corrupted.' Lee derided.

'By an infection like B.S.E., which will virtually reduce it to a sponge-like state, with similar cognitive abilities, but modern man has radically altered his respect for all animal and human life. Let me tell you that Monsanto genetically alters crops, so that they become resistant to the firm's very potent herbicide, Roundup. This means that farmers worldwide may now saturate their entire crop three days before harvest, killing only weeds and leaving the crop alive, but the fear is that the mass production of Roundup-Resistant crops will breed new strains of "super-weeds". In the U.S. alone, these deregulated R.R. crops include corn, soybeans, canola, cotton, sugar-beet, and alfalfa.'

'But maybe all that will alleviate hunger, in third-world countries, which are now plagued with crop infested parasites!' countered Lee.

'But that's only the thin edge of the wedge,' Lucy replied.

'In Kansas, for example, a firm called Ventrice Bioscience injected rice with human genes, because a potent anti-diarrhoea medicine can be extracted from this crop and routinely mixed with foods; it can even be put into so-called health-foods, like yoghurt and Granola. Also, goats injected with spider-genes can produce milk-proteins, which may be woven into bullet-proof vests. This makes a new type of lightweight vest, even stronger than the customary Kevlar body armour.'

Lee felt immersed in a sea of sententiousness as Lucy continued her diatribe.

'I see now that the Times newspaper reported recently that, "Humanity now stands at one of the greatest crossroads in history. Since twenty-sixteen scientists in the U.S. have begun implanting pigs and sheep with 'chimeric embryos' of human stem cells, to grow human organs like hearts and kidneys, for later transplantation into human beings." This work is still very controversial because the U.S. National Institute of Health is concerned that those human cells might migrate to the developing pig's brain, to make it in some way, more human.'

'Well,' laughed Lee, 'we might be able to breed a new generation of Franken-furters, which could tell us when they are properly cooked.'

'It's not funny, Lee,' retorted Lucy. 'Now scientists in Britain have been given permission to experiment with gene-editing, which will inevitably lead to designer babies. I fear they have now crossed the line, for the latest research permits them to harvest organs from living human embryos, but a recent law permits embryos to mature with the DNA of three people, so now we are saddled with three-parent families, and that is just the start of designer babies!'

Lucy's friend seemed upset, and changed the subject. 'Everyone knows why eggs are so cheap. The hens are squeezed into tiny wire cages, so small they can't even turn round. They have to wallow in their own waste for eighteen months and their feet rot, and their bones crumple, and their beaks get cut with red-hot irons so they cannot attack the others, sharing their cramped conditions.'

She continued. 'Chickens normally lay their eggs during daylight hours but the farmers are so devious that they wait until the Summer Solstice arrives, for the longest day of the year when it doesn't get dark until late evening. From then on they leave the overhead lights blazing until that time every day. Many chickens react to this, for they sense the abuse, and often smash their own eggs as soon as they are laid.'

Lee was horrified at all this new information, and decided he would now have to be really naïve to view animal welfare in the same light as the rest of the general public.

Lucy spoke up again, 'I used to work in turkey farms, and in factory farms with chickens, and I could tell you a few stories. In factory farming chickens and turkeys are selectively bred to grow so large, so fast, that they become crippled under their own weight. They are squeezed into cages so small they can't even spread their wings. Then they are killed either by gassing or being hung upside down to have their throats cut, or even dragged through an electric bath while they're still conscious.'

'That does seem very inhumane,' agreed Lee.

'Afterwards,' continued Lucy, 'they are injected with water to increase their body weight by at least twenty-per-cent. This is so they may be seen as a more robust product in the supermarkets; but water is not all they are filled with, for chemical additives like antibiotics and preservatives, are also introduced by an industrial process called vacuum tumbling.'

A sabber interrupted. 'You do realise that when a hen lays a fertilised egg it will hatch into a chicken;

you can tell the fertilised ones by the tiny spot of blood they contain, so they are actually foetuses, but the vast majority of the eggs that you eat are not fertilised. So what do you think they are?' she asked Lee.

'The start of a cheese omelette?' he joked.

'Well, think about it,' she replied; 'when the hen carries an unfertilised egg inside her, it's expelled as her menstrual matter. In fact, wild hens only lay about a dozen eggs a year, but modern hens have been intensively bred by genetic manipulation to lay up to three-hundred a year. So most of the eggs you eat are actually hens' periods. Did you know that there are thirty-five million hens, laying thirty million eggs a day in the U.K., but all egg production systems involve the killing of unwanted male chicks, one or two days after they hatch out. In the U.S. alone two-hundred and fifty million a year are put into the mincer just after birth.'

One of the others agreed, and confronted Lee. 'Do you even know what cheese is made from?'

Lee pleaded ignorance, so she continued.

'Permit me to enlighten you,' she loftily declared; 'cheese is made by separating milk into curds and whey. This is a process, requiring rennet, which contains an enzyme called Chymosin. There are very few cheeses, which may be made without rennet, which is normally obtained from the fourth stomach of a newly slaughtered calf, as adult cows do not possess this enzyme. Vegetarian cheeses are manufactured using rennet sourced from genetically-modified organisms.'

'Did you know, Lee,' said one of the sabbers, 'that all margarine is dyed to resemble butter?'

'Why would they need to do that?' queried Lee?'

'Because it's naturally more grey-looking than yellow. Let me tell you; margarine was first invented in 1869 by a Frenchman called Mége, from beef-suet. It is too soft at ambient temperature, so has to be plasticized for sale to consumers, but pure butter is far healthier than any margarine, most of which is emulsified and saturated with trans-fats.'

Lucy interrupted. 'Don't blind him with science. Let's just take him on a Sabb.'

She continued. 'We are going to invade a turkey farm in a few days, so why not come along, if you want to see for yourself.'

Lee was told this would be in the middle of the night so there was little chance of being caught, for all the workers would have gone home. He agreed to go along, but was to regret his decision.

The following Sunday evening he was picked up at midnight in a Transit van for the drive to East Anglia.

The group had set their sights on one of the most prestigious of farms, which charged one hundred pounds each, for a supposedly free-range turkey. These birds were Norfolk-Black turkeys, a choice breed destined for the tables of the wealthy, who were prepared to pay extra for animals they assumed were well treated.

As the group parked in a country lane near the turkey farm Lucy extracted a pair of bolt-cutters and everyone stumbled across the field in darkness, aware that using torches would draw unwanted attention.

When they reached the massive shed, with tiny windows near the roof, they asked Lee to cut the padlock, which he did easily.

He was told that some sheds cram in five thousand birds, and the noise is deafening. Someone produced a camcorder and attempted to video the scene, narrating a commentary, explaining that over the Christmas holidays in England ten million turkeys are slaughtered, and their carcass weight alone is over twenty-five thousand tons.

Lee was greeted by an image of abject misery; all the birds were covered with their own faeces, and many lay completely immobile on the filthy concrete, beside others, which seemed to have just died.

Those turkeys strong enough to stand upright were practically bald, with open wounds and weeping sores on their heads and backs. This was the result of cannibalism provoked by the stress of their habitat. Many had their beaks burned off in an effort to discourage this behaviour, which is caused when they get too fat to move and take their frustration out on their neighbours.

At least daylight could penetrate this stinking hellhole, and a door, at one end of the shed, could be opened for a spell during the day enabling the proprietors to legally claim the creatures had access to open ground, and fresh air. This alone granted them free-range status, but it was so dim inside that many of the birds were blind, and most could only stagger outside if they were desperate.

Most of the bedraggled creatures had no room for escape and blindly blundered about, climbing over their neighbours. This in itself was very painful for their feet were covered in ammonia burns, due to the build-up of excrement, but in turkey-terms these pathetic specimens were living in the lap of luxury. In reality, Lee was told, most of the ten million Christmas turkeys lived in conditions that made this place look like a five-star hotel.

They had closed the doors behind them when they ventured in, but someone had gone to collect the van, and now as they all climbed into the back, they left the shed doors wide open. As they made good their escape they could hear the commotion as thousands of turkeys stumbled into the freedom of the night. On the way home, they took the side roads, in case the police were alerted to their actions. Lucy told Lee that most ordinary turkeys are only allocated the same space as the roasting dish they will end up in, and never see daylight, or grass, or sunshine.

'They are the majority,' Lucy said, 'and are sold in places like supermarkets for as little as ten pounds each. Can you imagine the conditions that those poor creatures live in?' she asked. 'Even the general public, who often suspect this cruelty, have now been saturated by very expensive TV adverts from companies like Lidl. They show turkeys living in pristine open warehouses, layered in an abundance of clean, fresh hay and even foraging in wide open fields; plucking berries off trees and being fed fresh apples by the loving farmer, or should I say, ... actor, for this elaboration is obviously contrived; even having a glittering rainbow conveniently inserted into the background.'

As Lee contemplated the plight of the turkeys he had just freed, which were on sale for a hundred pounds each, he felt sick to his stomach, and now began to understand why some people become vegetarians.

He decided, there and then, that he would join this group, and to hell with the consequences. Somebody had to do something, for he was once told that evil prospers if good men do nothing.

The trouble was that Lee no longer considered himself a good man.

The group was still excited, chatting on their way home, although it was the middle of the night. They were talking about Sir Paul McCartney, who had just made a video stating that if slaughterhouses had glass walls, everyone would be vegetarian. He claimed absolutely nothing was wasted in the abattoirs, from noses to hooves.

They started planning their next venture, which involved a giant research laboratory in Beckanham, Kent. It had been revealed by a whistle blower at the site that thousands of small animals, like cats and dogs, and even monkeys were incarcerated and tortured there. This was for medical research and the vested interest of the cosmetic industry, which alone is responsible for the deaths of millions of cats and dogs every year, because as their publicity claims, ... 'You're Worth It.' Lee reflected that this statement was mainly aimed at their shareholders!

This whistle-blower, who was once employed in the facility, told horror stories of pigs being held down by ropes and emitting horrific squeals as they were bled to death.

He also told them of horses which were used to gather large quantities of blood.

'Why do they need so much blood,' Lee asked Lucy.

'Because they use it to grow viruses for immunisation against things like smallpox and polio, but I think there must be a better way.'

'I have seen horses with their necks all swollen with huge lumps, where a gallon of blood is often taken in one go. I have no idea how long they survive that treatment.' She then told the group, 'Pigs are also very intelligent creatures, having the cognitive abilities of a three-year-old human, but are kept in such horrific conditions that many simply go insane, from lack of stimulus. They are forced to produce litter after litter, giving birth in barren stalls without enough room to nuzzle their piglets.'

Lee was not amused, especially when he heard that in this facility toxic chemicals were dropped into rabbits' eyes to test the allergic reactions of shampoos and hair dyes.

'But why do they use rabbits for that?' - he queried.

'Because rabbits have no tear ducts, so cannot flush out the chemicals,' cried Lucy. 'Apparently the biggest cosmetic firm in the world issued a statement that they had ceased that practice, but it was later revealed that the individual ingredients of their shampoos were still being tested in rabbits' eyes.'

He also heard that fertilised eggs were injected with viruses, so that when the live chickens hatched out, they could be instantly crushed to preserve the virus for later use.

It was decided to write to other groups in the area, to devise a future plan of action. It had been realised years ago that not only were some of their phones being tapped, but also their text messages were recorded to gather evidence for potential prosecutions.

Lucy told Lee. 'We all change the SIM cards in our phones every week, because government agencies, like GCHQ and the FBI, are able to track not only the location of our mobile phones but can now send codes to any mobile to convert its microphone into a listening device; and may even turn the phone into a transmitter, now called a roving-bug. They don't even need to access the phone physically, but can enable it from some remote location, - even if the phone is switched off, and the only way to defeat this roving-bug ability, is to remove the phone battery! We discovered their covert operations utilise applications like "Sting-Ray" and "Fish-Hawk" to prey on us.'

The research facility at Beckanham was in its own expansive grounds, surrounded by fields where the horses were kept, so it seemed they would not have much trouble getting into the grounds. Gaining access to the buildings might prove more difficult.

'Will you help us, Lee?' asked Lucy.

'Okay …' he replied, 'what have I got to lose?'

'In for a penny, in for a pound,' said Lucy.

Lee reflected that he would never understand that expression, but now realised that there were a lot of things that he didn't understand.

CHAPTER TEN

Lee and Lucy lived close to each other, so they were dropped off together. Lucy was a casual dresser, like most of the group, but sported the odd piercing about her body. She had some tattoos on her arms, and other places, which Lee had yet to discover.

But tonight had been a tiring affair so she declined his offer of a nightcap at his flat. They were not instantly drawn to each other, but as Lee got to know her, he realised he was becoming greatly attracted by her demure demeanour.

He confessed that he currently had lots of problems and felt quite depressed. She laughed, and told him that she never worried about anything.

'What? ... not even bills, or fines!' he said in astonishment.

'Never paid a bill in my life,' she claimed. 'I just keep moving. A rolling stone gathers no debt,' she laughed. 'But if you are depressed and bored, I know a simple solution.'

Lee immediately thought his luck had changed, but it was not the case. She asked if he would come for a picnic with her out in the country. 'I have a moped and a spare helmet,' she told him.

'A picnic,' thought Lee, 'how boring!'

She continued, 'I know a place where we can find some magic mushrooms, out by the Community Village in Robertsbridge.'

Lee had heard of these hallucinogenic mushrooms before, but never of the village.

He wanted to get out of town and needed some female company, so he agreed to accompany her on her quest. They met up the following day and set off on the little moped. Lucy was a careful driver, and he felt safe, although his helmet seemed too tight. They reached Robertsbridge, about sixteen miles away from Hastings, in half an hour. Lucy claimed she knew the people at the Darvel Community Village, and had spent the odd day there, working in their workshop, which made nursery toys for countrywide distribution.

They were warmly greeted and escorted to where Lucy had once stayed with one of the resident families. The community consisted of a few hundred people, including dozens of families. They were not all related to each other but everyone was on very close terms, living, working and praying together, for it was a strict religious group. They were given dinner made from produce grown on their farmland. They had sheep but no cattle, yet were self-sufficient in feeding and clothing themselves. They wore simple clothes. The men mostly wore lumberjack style shirts, and jeans, while the women all wore long dresses. There was a conspicuous lack of jewellery, and

Lee noticed all the girls had long hair and didn't pluck their eyebrows, or wear make-up.

They were shown round the rustic wood-burning boilers, which supplied all their heating and hot water, just using wood gathered from their own forest. Each large house, of which there were many scattered about, housed two families on the ground floor and two above. The young unmarried men had their own quarters, as did the girls. Lee was instantly drawn to this simple way of life, where total commitment meant you lived there until you died. You were looked after, even during terminal illness, and buried in their own graveyard behind one of the fields.

They told Lee, 'If you feel a calling to join our community, you need to become a committed Christian, and be prepared to donate all your worldly goods to the centre for others to use. Individuals are not allowed to keep cars, but there are a couple of vehicles reserved for group transport.'

Lee wasn't committed to anything except staying alive; and the fact these people worked from early morning to night, six days a week for no wages, didn't appeal very much. Neither did the fact that phones, televisions and computers were prohibited, although there was a land-line in the office for emergencies. He certainly wouldn't get rich this way, Lee considered.

'We have no need of money here, unless we have to go into town, when we are given an allowance for our immediate needs. Nobody here goes hungry, or cold, or lonely and all the worries of the world like rent and bills are taken care of while you stay here, but you can leave whenever you want.'

Lucy and Lee thanked them for their profuse hospitality and wandered out of the fenced-in village, with its own gatekeeper's lodge and traffic barrier, neglecting to tell anyone they were off in search of magic mushrooms.

'That was like going back fifty years,' he remarked to Lucy.

'More like a hundred,' she responded.

They went to a field out of everyone's sight, and as Lucy predicted, there was an abundance of special mushrooms growing there, although the season for them was drawing to a close. The tiny mushrooms grew on thin stalks and were brown with a small nipple on top. Fortunately, Lucy had done this before and knew exactly what species to pick, for even Lee was aware of the dangers of toxic mushrooms, which could prove very deadly, very quickly.

They picked a few dozen and made their way back to the moped, which was left unlocked in the village. Soon they were back in Lee's flat, where Lucy brewed the mushrooms up in a teapot with a spoonful of Earl Grey tea.

After boiling for a few minutes she strained the liquid into two cups. She mixed in a large spoonful of organic honey and told Lee to just drink half, as he wasn't used to the effects, which would take thirty minutes to manifest. In the meantime, she suggested they visit the nearby garage and buy some flowers.

'It's important to have a pleasant, peaceful atmosphere, with good vibes,' she declared.

They returned from the garage shop, with two large bunches, which only cost a 'tenner', and put some relaxing guitar music on the stereo, while they waited for the effects to manifest. As Lee watched Lucy potter about his flat, he suddenly realised she would make a wonderful wife, being so considerate and guileless. She had displayed all the flowers beautifully, so the scene was set for their 'trip'.

'Why do you call it a trip?' queried Lee.

Lucy laughed and said, 'don't worry, you'll soon find out.' It didn't take long for that to happen.

They sat at the table, looking at the flowers, when Lee suddenly noticed the slender green stem of a tall blue Iris seemed to be sucking water up, as if breathing. It looked like the subtle shades of green, in its stem, were slowly changing. Lucy got up and walked over to where the carnations rested on the windowsill.

'Come and have a look at this, Lee,' she said softly. As he moved across the room he noticed that all the colours of his old carpet seemed so fresh it looked like someone had just cleaned it.

He stood and stared at a carnation. Everything else seemed normal, but the very petals of the flower started to slowly wriggle, with a life of their own. The rest of the flower seemed normal, but the petals themselves possessed their own individual energies.

'Do you see what I see?' she asked.

Lee certainly did, and remarked how he'd noticed pollen drift off the flower, in a cluster of tiny yellow dots when a slight breeze came through the window.

As he sat down again he watched Lucy as she crossed the room, and was stunned to see translucent auras of perfume cascade round her, like a misty vapour as she approached. He started to feel a bit panicky at this stage, until she held his hand and explained this was a normal reaction of having your senses and perception enhanced. As she squeezed his hand he looked down and noticed in amazement, minute sparkles of moisture exploding from his pores in rapidly continuous bursts of instant evaporation, oozing from the ends of his fingers.

'This is a continuous occurrence,' explained Lucy, 'which you normally cannot see in everyday life but when you're high you become much more aware of it. It's just perspiration, but now you can see it in minute detail.'

He was even more intrigued to notice that the harder he squeezed his thumb the quicker the sparkling pores opened and evaporated, until it seemed that the end of his thumb was totally soaked with moisture.

It wasn't all that Lee would see in detail that day. He examined the wooden table before him and saw that the wood grains were actually packed in very closely together, in perfectly straight lines but grew coloured and shaded as they extended in length, leaving overall patterns of grain which was all that the human eye would normally see.

Suddenly, Lucy brought a rose over to the table. He was intoxicated by the odour but drawn into the flower itself, because he saw ribbons of fine iridescent lines, like heavenly golden spiders' webs surrounding each petal, which swayed and oscillated to every sound and movement in the room.

He was unsure how long he was drawn into the flower, until Lucy came up and said, 'we must go outside, to give you a break. You're getting too deep into that, and I don't want to lose you. We should go outside, before it gets dark, for a little break.'

Lee didn't feel up to going outside. He had gone to his bathroom downstairs but had trouble getting out the door and finding his way back to the lounge. The whole world now seemed an alien place where he could be abandoned if he lost his way.

Luckily Lucy was there to guide him, and explained. 'You should never take a trip on your own, or you might not return.' ... Indeed: it was like visiting another planet. However, with Lucy's courage he ventured outside.

She suggested they eat something while walking down the road, because it would make them look more normal, but she told Lee to avoid staring at others, who would notice their eyes, now dilated like olives.

She searched for any fruit in the place, but all she could find were a couple of tomatoes. Lee didn't feel like eating, but agreed to copy Lucy's example.

When he bit into the tomato he couldn't believe it, for it tasted as succulent as the sweetest fruit he had ever eaten. He was now living in another world; a psychedelic world.

As they came out of the flat he noticed all the cars were luminescent with a different spectrum of colour, which he had never seen before. They were glowing and flowing with colour and grace, and he could almost sense the personality of their designers in the different models. Some vehicles looked aggressive, while others confident, or even innocuous, but each shone in its own magical cloak. They walked towards the park, passing a dog lying inside a shop window.

As daylight was almost too much to bear, they were wearing dark glasses, which helped shield them from public scrutiny. The dog in the window was a bitch, which had recently had a litter of pups, and she was sprawled out while some of the pups suckled her. Lee was amazed because not only could he sense the pecking order of the brood, but could actually see just how happy and proud this dog was, garnering total contentment from the attention of her offspring.

A group of punks came sauntering towards them, and Lee felt a bit nervous, but as they approached he couldn't help but burst out laughing, for it was so obvious to him just how proud the leader was, swaggering down the street with his leather jacket and orange hair. Lee now realised, that in his current state, he could tell if other people were vain or shy, or aggressive, or timid.

They picked a quiet road to bring them to the park. They had to be careful crossing roads, but they were able to hear cars coming from afar, and indeed, had to wait ages until they 'swooshed' past, with effortless grace. This park was never locked as it had too many entrances, but as it was growing dark and there was nobody about, they made their way into the centre which was quite sheltered.

They had paused to gaze at a tiny, ornate metal windmill. Near the device Lee was astonished to see the tiniest spots of rust flaking off as it spun. He stood amazed, listening to every small creak and groan of the mechanism, which seemed to possess a life of its own, where every nut and bolt played a part.

Lee was also shocked to notice, in the fading light, the multi-coloured shades of trees, in colours his mind had never seen before. He tried to enlighten Lucy about the rich variety of colour he was seeing, but she explained. 'We all see different colours differently, even in everyday life. Do you accept that you might see green, for example, in a slightly different shade than I do?'

'Okay,' Lee agreed.

'So,' she continued, 'by that reckoning your shade of green, or indeed any colour, is dictated to you by the person who first points it out, and teaches you the name of that specific colour, although that individual might see that particular shade completely differently to you; and in fact they might be encountering completely different shades to the ones that you sense, but the relevant name you learn to call any specific shade stays with you for the rest of your life.

So you might see green, in the same shade that they see red, for example. It depends on the physical make-up of your eye and how an individual's brain interprets the radiation of the different colours, which send out different vibrations, even if you can't normally see them. This is why ultra-violet, which is bluer than blue, can burn and blind you, although you cannot see it.

However, bees and many other creatures can see it, and may possibly perceive many more colours than us.

The human iris can distinguish between ten million colours, and every individual iris has over two hundred unique characteristics that can identify a person much more reliably than a fingerprint. Who knows, maybe great artists simply possess an enhanced colour spectrum, as opposed to the rest of us. Perhaps all those poor souls who suffer from depression may be sensually limited by a lack of colour, in the world that they normally perceive.'

'That's heavy,' Lee responded, 'but I love my shade of colours, even when I'm not high.'

'Look at the stars, Lee,' said Lucy, as the sky grew dark. He stood still and stared at the heavens, exposed as never before. They lay above him, not as a flat canopy but as a multi-layered dimension, which escalated into different levels of infinite distance.

'I can actually see how far forwards or backwards each individual star is positioned, and how bright some are compared to others,' he told her. The sky was no longer a blanket but a three-dimensional infinity. He saw that all the stars were specifically spaced and layered, relating one to another in depth and distance and brightness. He had never seen anything so intoxicating in his whole life. Suddenly, he felt himself swaying, and wondered why. He looked at Lucy, and all was normal again, until he stared up once again, transfixed by the banquet of beauty spread before him.

Again, he felt slightly dizzy but suddenly realised the reason. It looked like the heavens were moving, but in fact he now realised that it was the Earth ... as he stood still on it. He was now able to sense the infinitesimal rotation of the world he lived on, and he was moved to tears.

'Lucy,' he cried, 'I can feel the Earth move.'

'I know,' she replied, 'just like in the song.'

He then stared at the pebbled pathway where many thousands of little stones in varied sizes, were randomly scattered, except now they were not scattered. His brain was able to see elaborate patterns, combining with each other to paint multi-coloured mosaics of perfect design, all different but distinctly relating one to another in perfect sequence. It seemed that nothing in life was random, but fell into specific boundaries of clinical composition.

They lay down by the river to watch the ducks settle in for the night and were able to see the pecking order within the group, in the same fashion they had noticed with the dog and her pups. As they lay flat on the grass he whispered to Lucy, 'what is that rustling noise. Can you hear it as well?'

'What you're hearing Lee, is the sound of plants and stuff slowing closing up, to rest for the night,' she laughed. It was getting chilly as night drew in, and Lee wished he had worn his jacket. He looked at his arms and suddenly noticed each individual hair on his skin rise and fall, as if to gather a pocket of air to keep warm. This was actually what normally happened in everyday life, but he had never witnessed the process before. It was magical to realise just how complicated, yet controlled, were the mechanisms of the human body, and life in general.

Time itself took on a new perspective and before they knew it, they were back home together in the warmth and security of the little flat. Lucy decided to make a cup of tea, but warned Lee to make sure it was not too hot when he drank it.

'Remember, our senses are heightened and you will feel things much more intensely.'

As the kettle boiled, they laughed; for as it came to the boil it sounded just like an old-fashioned steam engine. Lee dropped a spoon on the floor, but as he bent down to pick it up, he couldn't believe his eyes.

The cheap old linoleum, which was almost worn out, sparkled in multi-coloured effervescence. The pattern comprised many thousands of coloured dots, sprayed on in layers, and when he stared at it he could see the order in which the specific layers had been sprayed on, and the way they lay on top of each other. He felt like he was up in space, looking down on clusters of cities, glowing with millions of lights, but his eyes were able to focus on each and every one of them.

Lucy turned the stereo on and Lee went up close to the speakers, for he could see clusters of reddish dots forming swirling patterns in tune to the music. As he stared at the patterns of sound he went even closer, putting his head against the speaker enclosure, except it wasn't there; it seemed to disappear as he got drawn into it, and he felt the box itself was starting to enfold him. Lucy could see he was losing it and rushed over to pull him away.

'So you see the music, Lee! That's okay,' she told him. 'Keep calm, I can see it too, - it's normal,' she said.

It seemed more miraculous than normal to Lee, but he accepted a set of headphones, which Lucy gently placed over his ears.

'Check this out,' she squealed in joy, as he listened to the Beatles song, "Lucy in the Sky with Diamonds" which, she knew, correlates to L.S.D.

She studied his reaction, which switched from pure mindless ecstasy to confusion, as he suddenly tore off the headset ... 'Now I can understand every word of that song, but it's too much beauty, right inside my head.'

Lee felt his reaction must be similar to going mad, when too much stimuli saturated and overwhelmed the brain.

Just then the phone rang. It was a reverse charge call. He couldn't decide to accept it or not, for paranoia was creeping in, demanding a solution. Then, as he prevaricated he heard in amazement the line of operators in the telephone exchange responding to a multitude of varied calls. He was hearing every detail of every conversation from emergency calls to directory enquiries, and was able to distinguish between them all with clarity. He slammed the phone down in panic.

'We must drink lots of fluid, Lee, or we'll dehydrate,' said Lucy giving Lee a cup of lukewarm tea. As he raised it he could see a red glow where the cup had been on the table.

'That must be really hot ... you've burnt my table,' he complained. Lucy came over and asked him to place his hand on a glass shelf.

This was very cold to the touch, so he took his hand away immediately, but was stunned to see a perfect outline of his palm and fingers, down to the finest detail.

'What you see now is infra-red,' said Lucy, without elaboration.

'Why can't we be like this all the time?' he asked.

'Some people believe that we do actually inherit those senses at birth,' she replied, 'and that babies with their big bright eyes possess all these senses and can actually see auras - but those senses leave us after a few months. Animals usually retain some, and I believe they can see auras all the time. However, human beings wouldn't last long in this world if they remained as sensitive as that all the time.'

Lee was now exhausted mentally but not physically. He went and lay on the bed, but began to realise how very sexual he now felt. He touched his hand and felt the flow of sensuality emanating from it which made him feel even more aroused. He found he couldn't resist the feel of his own skin, never mind that of Lucy's, who had lain down beside him on the bed.

He was much older than his companion, but he sensed they now shared a strong empathy. They reached out to grasp each other's hands, indulging in the luxury of pristine touch and feeling. It was a magical moment, for he knew she felt the same way. After the first embrace they threw caution to the wind and explored each others' bodies in an ecstasy of mindless abandonment. He felt that this was the first time he had really made love to a woman and pitied lesser mortals, grasping more meagre fulfilment.

It was only then when they were both spent, ... their minds still racing and raging with stimuli, that Lee realised, lying exhausted unable to sleep, why this experience is called a trip. It is impossible to escape your senses, even though you desperately want to; you have embarked on a journey: a journey where some creator is saying, 'You want to see me? Well, now you do ... so sit there and deal with it.'

As he lay there, Lee reflected that life was obviously a lot more complicated than he first thought. He now had to consider that there might just be some form of Deity, controlling the Universe. He spent the next few hours, wide awake, wrestling with that possibility.

CHAPTER ELEVEN

It took Lee a few days to revert to the mundane routine of his prosaic little world, for he was now unsure of what was real in life and what was not.

However, he and Lucy had decided they were now soul-mates, and because he had promised to look after her, he agreed to accompany her to the research laboratories without being aware of the risk involved.

They set off that Sunday evening when no staff would be on the premises. They knew there would be a watchman on duty, so one of the group was designated to keep an eye on the guard seconded in his gatehouse, and any patrols or movements would be relayed to the sabbers by walkie-talkie. They parked up where the security guard could be seen, sitting in his little office with a portable television flickering in the background, but he was fast asleep with his feet propped on the desk. Their driver, who was keeping watch with the walkie-talkie, was only to use it if the guard came out of the cubicle or tried to use the telephone.

The remaining group of six made their way from the van, to the fields, before reaching the horse enclosure. They didn't need bolt-cutters at this stage for the wire-net fence was easily snipped with wire-cutters. The group skirted past the horses, which all seemed asleep, standing upright.

Everybody moved as quietly as possible and, at the other side of the enclosure, cut another hole in the fence. They were now into the compounds housing the main facilities. They had been supplied by the whistle-blower with a rough map of the huge layout, and deliberately entered the block furthest away from the gatehouse. The two-way radios were still silent for the moment.

Someone had purchased cheap torches with red covers over the lenses, as these reflected little light. The group had intended to purchase some night-vision goggles from an army surplus store, but currently could only afford torches, and petrol for their old van.

Lucy gave Lee the bolt-cutters to gain entry to a large building with double doors. They had agreed to spy out the layout before deciding which animals to release. This would need some co-ordination, as the noise and commotion of hordes of creatures released at the same time would awaken the dead, let alone the security guard.

They filed quietly into a long warehouse, where hundreds of small wire cages were stacked up to six feet high either side of the main corridor. They housed chickens, which immediately awoke and started screeching, as the group made their way along a dark, dank corridor. The noise grew louder the further they penetrated into the rows of cages, but Lee kept his ear tuned to the radio, convinced that the whole world would soon hear the ruckus. They quickly made their way out of the chicken compound, convinced there was nothing they could do to help these captives, so they decided that the next best option would be to release the monkeys. When they broke into this building they were surprised to find it contained a number of doorways to various sections. They found one packed with dogs, and another crammed with cats. Many of the creatures seemed stir-crazy for they relentlessly paced and scraped against the bars of their cages; in similar fashion to their brethren, kept in public zoos. They decided to release the dogs last, as they would probably make more noise, although everyone was surprised to find these dogs didn't bark, but just seemed to emit husky gasps.

Lucy explained, 'All these dogs have been de-barked, by what is known as a vocal-cordectomy, so the technicians can work on them in relative peace and quiet.'

They continued to free the cats, which were just secured by simple bolts on their cages. The cats clustered together, but three of the girls herded them out into the fresh air, where they simply scattered in different directions.

Feeling flushed with success the group proceeded to the far end of the complex building, where they eventually found the monkeys behind another secure door. They were warned that some of the monkeys would be infected with viruses, so they were very careful in letting them loose, one by one.

They made sure an open door was visible to the creatures, before poking the bolts open with a broom handle. This task was down to Lee, while the rest of the group huddled in a corner to avoid panicking the creatures. As each cage door was opened, the creatures immediately leapt out and scampered straight out the double-doors, which were illuminated by the lights of the compound. The monkeys were so fast nobody had time to see where they went, but Lee was glad he had brought along his thick industrial gloves, for a single bite from one of these animals might have proved fatal. None of the group had considered the danger to the public, or of the hassle the authorities would have in trying to re-capture them, or the fact that many would have to be shot if they presented a hazard.

The final job was releasing the dogs. The creatures were so excited they jumped all over the group of sabbers, who panicked and decided to leave as quickly as possible, but some of the girls had discovered rabbits stacked in a dim quarter of the block. They were almost in total darkness, but it didn't matter, for these rabbits were mostly blind with blank squid-like eyes staring into blackness. The girls came back and declared that nothing could be done for the poor creatures.

Just then the radio crackled a warning, so they had to leave immediately, taking a different route out. They quickly made their way round the side of the building, but noticed that in the adjacent building multitudes of tiny cages housing rats and mice. By the long bench in this facility were a number of cigar cutters, screwed to the wooden counters.

Lucy declared, 'those are used to decapitate the poor bastards. Quick ... but messy!'

The group then made their way past the horse compound, arguing about whether or not to free the animals. They had to make a quick decision, for the radio told them the guard was now on the phone, presumably to the police.

'Where would these horses go - they are in such a bad state they wouldn't get very far, and it's easy to spot a horse,' argued Lucy.

Lee agreed. 'They are better off here, because although they won't live long they will get medical attention to keep them alive as long as possible. After all, horses don't come cheap.'

The van had circled round and picked them up minutes later, as they left the fields. In the rush Lucy dropped the bolt-cutters, but they didn't have time to find them in the dark. Driving down the road they spotted one of the monkeys under the light of a street-lamp, digging up some plant in a nearby garden, and everybody laughed hysterically.

'Maybe he's into gardening,' cried Lucy, 'for after all, he shares about ninety-nine per-cent of our human genes,' she laughed. 'Seriously, though, are you aware that common chimps in laboratories can be taught to use sign language and computer keyboards, and it is now generally accepted that higher primates can learn to sign and communicate with humans. Some of them can teach others, in their group, complicated sign language; even tapping out consecutive numbers, flashed onto screens, faster than the humans who taught them that technique.'

The group then headed for the nearby town of Bromley, just minutes away, where they parked outside an all-night venue. They stayed there until dawn, when they felt it was safe to drive home in the morning rush-hour. They got back to Hastings without incident, and Lee and Lucy went to bed together, but they were so tired they both went to sleep immediately.

A few days later Lee got a call from the leader of the group. He was told that Lucy had been arrested at her flat, for her DNA had been matched to bolt-cutters, which police had discovered in a field near the facility. They had also captured pictures from Bromley CCTV of the number plate of the Transit van, and although they searched for the driver, he avoided arrest by fleeing to the south of Ireland.

Everyone was too scared to visit Lucy as they didn't know what she might have let slip to the police. She was given a public defender, but bail was refused. Lee was shattered. Every time things seemed to be getting better, his life went into a downward spiral. Now his latest love would also end up in prison for a long time, as he knew the courts would make her an example to others as a deterrent.

He felt he had to get away for a while, so arranged to spend a couple of days with Tom in the countryside.

Tom made him very welcome, but Lee told him as little as possible, just mentioning that he needed a break for he was having a challenging time at the moment.

They both shared an interest in building small models, but Tom preferred Meccano sets, whereas Lee used simple matchsticks. Lee was fascinated to see the elaborate cranes and railway engines that Tom had spent years building. They all had electric motors in them and functioned like the real thing. Some were built to scale and mounted on miniature railway tracks, although they couldn't go very far. On occasion Tom would take them to exhibitions, but could only squeeze one or two in his car at a time.

He showed Lee his latest purchase, a small radio-controlled drone, with four little propellers and a tiny camera mounted underneath. The controlling handset had a small screen, which enabled the user to see exactly what the drone camera saw as it flew overhead. Tom said he found it on the internet for only a hundred quid. He knew that Lee's old hobby was kite-flying and told him he could borrow the drone for a while.

This gadget was to prove extremely useful to Lee in the coming days.

However, Tom could see his friend was stressed out, and told Lee about a place where anyone could go for a week of quiet contemplation. These were called retreats, he explained, and this one was situated on the Isle of Wight, just a couple of hours from Hastings. He said it would take a few days to book him into the place, called Quarr Abbey, where the cost of his food and accommodation would be covered, as the Benedictine monks who ran the guesthouse only requested voluntary donations of whatever their guests could afford. Lee jumped at the opportunity, but decided to visit La-Lu first, as he waited for the booking to be confirmed. She had taken her final vows and was now able to receive one or two visits a year. He telephoned the convent and spoke to the Mother Superior, who reluctantly agreed that La-Lu's old friend could come and pay his respects for a couple of hours.

He would be given tea while he was there, but smoking was prohibited and he could only speak to La-Lu through a metal grill. Naturally, no physical contact would be possible. Furthermore, he must not speak to any other nuns he chanced to meet on his visit. It was arranged that Lee would visit the following weekend. As it was Thursday he didn't have long to wait and managed to book a cheap train ticket the same day.

The weekend came quickly, but Tom rang and told him he would have to wait some weeks for his retreat, as the guesthouse at the Abbey was full until then.

Lee had drawn some money from his account for the trip to see La-Lu and for his retreat in the Abbey, but he was still very careful with his finances as he planned to use the remaining funds to return to China, guessing he might need to leave the country quickly.

He also realised this would probably be the last time he would see his long-lost love and, as he boarded the train for London, felt a lump in his throat. It was the same sensation he had felt after the Old Bailey court case when he said goodbye to La-Lu as she was being taken off to prison.

When he negotiated the chaos of the London mainline station he went straight down to the Underground, where he had to study a wall map for his destination and finally managed to work out which line to get on, and how many stops before his destination. He found that early afternoon on the tube was even more daunting than the rush-hour, for people opposite seemed to be staring. During the rush-hour he could avoid their gaze while standing up but, on sitting down, now felt he was the focus of attention. He just couldn't wait for this journey to end, and was even tempted to get out and board the next train but he didn't have the time.

He managed to make it to the convent in time for his meeting, and was ushered into a sparse, clinical waiting room. The Prioress gave him an austere greeting, appearing uneasy in male company. He was informed that La-Lu was now known as Sister Marion, and would retain that title for good. Lee was too intimidated to ask any questions so after a few preliminaries was led into a little room, with a bench facing a small perforated grill, in the opposite wall.

He had to wait a few minutes for Sister Marion to appear, and when she did, he barely recognized her for she wore a full habit, and had lost weight. He found it difficult to see her features through the fine mesh of the grill but they could hear each other quite clearly.

She informed him that anything they discussed would be in total confidence, so he told her all about Ping's demise, and the fact he had been handsomely compensated for the injury which Ping had inflicted. He even told her about the accident on the towpath and the tragic incident at the farm. She had no news of these things, as contact with the outside world was strictly limited in the convent.

She told Lee he had blood on his hands and needed to repent, or he would sink deeper into sin.

'We must forgive all the people and all the wrongs that happened to us at the orphanage, Lee, because we are the only ones still suffering, for the perpetrators won't even remember our names. Carrying hate and revenge for some evil is pointless, because one form of hate will only feed another, and there are two ways people actually hurt you. Firstly, by the execution of the act itself and secondly by the memory, which will remain to haunt you; but forgiving someone is like deciding to free a prisoner: then discovering that prisoner was actually you!

I know you ache inside, Lee, but ask God to grant you the strength and compassion to forgive; only then will you be free to start your life again.'

Lee expected this reaction, but what did surprise him was that La-Lu promised to pray daily for his redemption, as she worried greatly about the fate of his soul. She told him that nuns do a lot of praying, and every morning a priest would visit the convent to celebrate mass, which Lee gathered was the high point of the day.

Much of her day was taken up by chores but as this was a contemplative Dominican Order, no-one was allowed out except in exceptional circumstances. The only news received in the convent were letters from close relatives, which had to be strictly censored, as the nuns could only respond to emergencies.

She explained that her life was now run on a strict timetable, and entailed regular visits to the chapel five times a day, when devotions and prayers were recited for an hour at a time, but singing hymns in church was prohibited, except at Christmas, when they could indulge in carol singing. Lee suggested he could send her money but she explained that her final vows included poverty, chastity and obedience, so she could not accept his kind offer.

Lee realised he was now out of the picture regarding any future relationship between himself and La-Lu.

It also looked as though this would be a permanent state of affairs, for she seemed blissfully content in her new life, and had even received a full remission of her prison sentence for her previous crimes.

She admitted she did not find the routine of the convent easy, being woken in the middle of the night to pray with others in the cold chapel, but confessed she had never had much discipline in her former life.

She told him Mother Superior was very strict, as she had been there nearly fifty years, but that the Prioress was sympathetic and had taken her under her wing. She told Lee that silent, unquestioning obedience was the order of the day and that when she took her final vows she had to lie down in a coffin in the chapel to show she had died to the world; but that she would be propped up in that same coffin, when she physically died, to show the world that she now lived in heaven.

She told Lee he would be wise to go on his retreat, and should seek salvation as soon as possible.

Lee didn't bother to enlighten her to the fact that the main reason for this retreat was an attempt to escape justice for all his wrongdoings, which were slowly catching up on him. He heard a bell tinkle behind La-Lu, informing her there were only five minutes left. She took this time to explain to Lee that because of his crimes she must avoid all future contact with him until he redeemed himself. She explained that she found the memory of their past lives very painful, and it was probably best that they now went their separate ways.

Lee was offered some refreshments for the journey home, but he declined, feeling that these people had brainwashed his lifelong friend, convincing her to have nothing more to do with him in future.

He left the convent without looking back, realising that he would never see La-Lu again, for she would now try to forget all about him.

The journey home was uneventful, and he was glad to be secure again behind the locked door of his little flat. There was a letter from Tom telling him to get ready immediately for his retreat, as a cancellation had come through for the following day, and his journey to the Island was now booked. He rang Tom to thank him, and casually mentioned he needed to acquire an English driving licence, for he remembered the café group were now without a driver or any transport. Tom promised to make enquiries on his behalf.

CHAPTER TWELVE

Lee caught the early train at Warrior Square station and arrived at Portsmouth Harbour, three hours later, having changed at Brighton.

He had a cup of coffee and a croissant for breakfast at the ferry terminal and noted that the boats ran every hour.

Before the huge ferry docked he had time to admire the stunning Spinnaker tower building adjacent to the terminal. Clusters of foot passengers were initially allowed to board, followed by clattering trucks, which took up the bottom deck. There were more decks above for the scores of cars, waiting patiently in regimented lanes. Loading and checking the cargo gave the passengers enough time to scuttle to the top deck, where drinks and snacks could be purchased before the boat sailed.

As Lee was one of the first on board he secured a prime spot in the queue and was served quickly, enabling him to pick a window seat, facing forward. Unfortunately, as the ferry left port it swivelled around so he ended up facing the mainland for the journey. He eventually decided to go out on deck and stand in the wind and sunshine to admire the approaching island and soon spotted the tall spire of the abbey, which seemed to be the biggest landmark.

It only took forty minutes before the boat was docking at Fishbourne.

This was a tiny hamlet with a small pub and the ferry terminal, placed next to a sandy beach, bordered only by some rather exclusive houses.

The terminal was less than a mile from the abbey and he relished the walk along the country road. He had seen the tall spire of the abbey from the boat, but nevertheless was pleasantly surprised to gaze at its grandeur, as he plodded up the long path from the main road. The silence struck him as he escaped the noise of the traffic, so he decided to venture into the church, which was open from morning to night, to bask in its calm solitude.

For some reason, unbeknown to himself, Lee always relished the peaceful cold tranquilities of churches and graveyards. Indeed, his only walks in London were not through Soho, but into the many churches and graveyards dotted about. Maybe, he reflected, he was drawn to their marble-cold promise of oblivion.

He left the church, which was lit only by a single candle glowing beneath a magnificent ornate globe of pure gold. This was the precious church monstrance and was held aloft on chains, ready to be lowered during Mass.

On leaving, he spotted the gatekeeper's door. It was unobtrusive and set aside from the main entrance. When he rang the bell his heart sank, for it was quite some time before an elderly monk, dressed in the lengthy black habit of the Benedictine order came to the door and greeted him warmly.

'Are you booked in?' he queried. When Lee confirmed this, the monk inquired if the small bag, which Lee carried, was his only luggage. Lee was shown up a few flights of stairs to a lovely little room shaped like a rotunda.

'Do you mind bells?' asked the old monk.

'No! ... well ... I hope you don't get too disturbed because you are right under the clock tower.'

Lee assured him he would be fine, but the guest-master then told him the person who had booked in before him had just left, as apparently the clock had disturbed him during the night.

This explained why Lee was able to secure a place so quickly, so he couldn't complain even if he wanted to, but this was before he realised that the clock wound itself up, to crank out chimes every thirty minutes.

He was tired and lay down, having been told that he would hear the dinner bell in about an hour. He slept, but not for an hour because he was aroused by the half-hourly clang of the huge bell above him. It was the stirring of the mechanism that woke him, as it clicked and clucked, seeming to clear its throat, before announcing to the world that it was still alive and would not be ignored.

Before dinner he queued in the barren cloister, adjacent the dining hall, or refectory. He greeted the other guests of four young men and an old blind chap. The guest-master asked him how he got on with the clock, and Lee told him it was louder than he expected.

'Treat it like an old friend and you'll soon get used to it,' came the cheery reply.

Lee wasn't sure he wanted to get used to it, but the conversation ended as the monk explained that nobody talked once inside the refectory and guests could only communicate by hand gestures, and had to take turns serving themselves the food. The daily exception to this routine was when tea was served in the annex, when Father Prior and Father Abbot liked to meet and chat with their guests.

The guests then filed silently into a huge long room, where a massive table, in the middle of the room, was laid out with place names.

The visitors sat facing each other, while two lines of monks sat some distance apart, with their backs against two bleak stone walls, facing either side of the guest table.

Father Abbot presided regally, at his own separate table at the top of the room and led the group in offering Grace. There was a pulpit of sorts halfway down the long room, where a solitary monk overlooked the proceedings. As the guests served each other, this sombre black figure placed a large book on the lectern.

'We will continue today's reading from the life of Saint Francis of Assisi,' he announced.

His was the only voice to be heard for the rest of the meal. He proceeded to relate how St. Francis, the son of a nobleman, forsook his heritage, took a vow of poverty and founded the order of the Franciscans.

'It was widely believed this man could commune with animals and revered nature as much as he did God.'

The repast was sumptuous, being produce grown organically, and tended to by the monks in their own gardens. Lee was confused when he saw there was no meat on the table but then realised these monks were probably all vegetarians. As it proved, his assumptions were correct. The guests adjourned to the annex room where they were shortly joined by the Abbot and the Prior. It was very informal, and everyone gave a brief synopsis of where each of them lived and what sort of lifestyle they pursued. Most of the men cited various qualifications from various institutions, which were acknowledged with silent approval, and a nodding of heads.

One guest seemed to be some sort of celebrity for when he mentioned he was in the music business, two of the others acknowledged they had recognised him as the lead singer in some sort of boy-band. One of the guests even claimed to have purchased some of his music. He positively purred at this acknowledgement of fame, but their comments were meaningless to the monks, who scorned all worldly values. Lee suddenly realised that this particular guest was the young man he had encountered while working in the hotel in Hastings; the very individual he had repeatedly refused to serve, that evening.

As luck would have it, this boy did not recognise him and was totally dumbfounded when it became Lee's turn to distribute some Baklava desserts, in the refectory. For some strange reason the boy missed out on this tasty treat when Lee passed him by, but as silence ruled the room, there was little he could do about it.

As other individuals were drawn into the conversation Lee was asked where he hailed from, and what attracted him to Quarr.

'Well, it's not the clock, that's for sure,' he quipped. 'I've had a challenging time recently, in recovering from a *slight* drug addiction.'

Lee figured this would curtail any further inquisition, and he was correct, for the other guests never spoke to him again.

They generally avoided his company as he wandered about the beautiful forest grounds where only monks and guests were permitted to roam. These woods led directly to the beach which Lee followed for a mile into Fishbourne, where he went into the quaint little pub and indulged in a fresh crab sandwich, washed down by a glass of cider.

The next day the guest master visited him in his room, hoping he had had a pleasant night's sleep. Lee was unable to confirm this, but was somewhat mollified when he was informed that another guest was due to check out the following day, so he should be able to switch rooms.

Lee had gone to the morning mass, as services were not simply for Catholics, although most of the guests followed that tradition. He was able to sit with the monks on the wooden pews facing the elevated altar. There was a small flock of faithful parishioners assembled in the recesses of the cavernous church, and they proved to be regulars at all the services, some of which Lee found very moving.

There was Benediction, Compline, Prime and Vespers - the latter being held in total darkness. This was the last order of the day, and once the monks had herded around the altar, candles were extinguished as Lee and the others sat with bated breath in the cold dark of the locked church while the monks broke into melodious Gregorian chants. He had never heard such moving devotions, and Lee wondered if he was the only one there with tears streaming down his face. In the darkness nobody moved but he suspected the others reacted in the same way, for he could sense an occasional hand rising to wipe a face. He couldn't fathom why he found it such an emotional experience, but the novelty never wore off during his stay there.

As the clock above him clanked into action during the night, Lee was woken every half-hour. At one point he decided to join the monks as they rose to pray in the middle of the night. The guests were told they were always welcome to join in night prayers as the church doors were locked to the public and total privacy prevailed.

He got dressed and made his way downstairs to where he was greeted by silence from a queue of monks awaiting their Abbot, who soon arrived to guide his flock down the long ancient stone cloisters, lit only by dim candles. It was a surreal experience for Lee, immersed in this alien world where he quietly trekked along with the others in the dark confines of the chapel amidst the dead of night.

As he relaxed in the darkness, he mused that this was not something he would normally do, but a singular experience he should always remember.

An amusing incident occurred the following day. They all awoke to a clutter of press photographers outside the monastery entrance, so Lee ventured into the gardens for some peace and quiet, but was confronted by a young girl who enquired where she could find the 'monkey house'. He directed her to the main office.

As he returned to the monastery he saw that a horde of young girls in the briefest of skirts, … barely crowning their fleshy abundance, had gathered outside and were hassling the monks. They were hoping to meet their idol, whom the press had discovered was hibernating inside the monastery.

There was a short standoff, until a limousine drew up in the courtyard and their famous guest made a swift exit with his entire luggage.

Monastic orders do not relish legions of lecherous groupies on their doorstep, and Lee noted this gaggle of nubile wenches seemed to upset the monks' routine and equilibrium. Later he learned that this celebrity had donated a hi-tech music centre to the order as an apology, but the monks donated it to a local charity, which collected the item the next day.

The guest-master, who had taken a liking to him, often visited Lee in his new room. They had many soul-searching conversations into the late hours, when he bestowed his wisdom on Lee, who drank it in like nectar for the wise old priest sensed Lee was a troubled soul.

As a father confessor, he gently probed Lee's troubled mind, sensing his sadness. It was the lingering pain of unrequited love regarding La-Lu, whom he felt he had let down and deserted. Lee was told the best way to exorcise such dilemmas was to confess to a confidante, and pour out his innermost feelings, because in any sort of confession priests are bound by sacred oaths of silence. He asked Lee to describe in detail the lady in question.

Lee explained about the events leading up to La-Lu's joining the convent.

Lee told him. 'When we worked together, she would only have to come near, or enter a room, for me to become deliriously happy; to the point where I just started giggling, I was so happy: but thinking back I fear she thought I was laughing at her. The trouble was, that when she looked at me I got so intoxicated I couldn't contain myself, and found I could scarcely breathe in her presence. Even a glance from her offered peace and hope and trust, and every word from her lips, a promise from heaven. I was so enraptured by love that I felt no two hearts in history could rival our union.

I sensed such love could touch me only once, even if I lived a million lifetimes and died a million deaths. I felt she was my single soul-mate, chanced upon and chosen by fate from billions of souls walking the Earth.'

Lee then explained the religious transformation that La-Lu undertook, and how he then sank into depression and self-loathing.

The old monk explained. 'In a sense we are all animals, but rational animals, waging a constant dialogue with our environment and our Creator, as we strive for perfection; but you were just chasing a kind of dream, … my son.

Such perfection does not, and cannot exist on this Earth, but we have to explore many concepts before the realisation surfaces that perfection in this world is only an illusion.

Otherwise, there would be no purpose in any single life and death would hold no sting. As children we grow up fearless, and the concept of death is irrelevant; yet as life numbs us to reality we still search for happiness, which at best is fleeting.

Life, even at its very best, is not a joyous game of chance but is full of sadness. This is the only kind of world a God would create for his creatures; a world full of suffering and injustice, where man would be forced to turn to Him, usually on bended knees. Just remember, very bad things will happen to good people, and good things will happen to very bad people.

Anything else would be senseless, for then we would not need a creator, and would just end up believing in ourselves and not God.'

The old man continued, 'Do not strive for love or peace or pity, and certainly not for health or wealth, for they are all temporal. Everything we achieve in life is transient, for we all play at the table of chance. You just have to play the hand you are given, and everyone gets a different deal. We all play for people or power or property, forgetting that we must leave that table one day, for someone else to take our place, when all our possessions and winnings pass to a third party. In a hundred years few people will even remember our name, and most traces of our lives here will reside only in the mind of God, where we will exist for ever.'

Lee listened as the old boy continued. 'Anger and frustration will always slumber within you, Lee, to vent its rage like a sleeping volcano unless you come to terms with your God and yourself.

Strangely enough, this is not as simple as forgiving others, but is more about forgiving yourself and remembering that God's greatest gift is free will, giving you the opportunity to acknowledge your Creator and choose eternal life in the hereafter.'

Lee was advised to surrender his desires to God at the start of every new day, asking for blessings on the people he would meet, and even the food that he would eat.

He should give thanks not just for what he had, but also for the things that existed in this world, that he didn't, or couldn't have.

His mentor continued. 'Do you not realise, my boy, that even if you got everything you wanted in life, you would have nothing left to strive or hope for, and would be just as miserable as ever. Nobody on Earth is truly successful, for we all make great mistakes in life, because we all possess fallible human natures, and the richer we get, the more selfish we become.

Remember, Lee, it is still a beautiful world even if you cannot grasp or understand it. Even people who knew they would soon be put to death, have scratched poems on the walls of concentration camps to the praise and glory of God.'

The old monk continued. 'One renowned poem was found on the wall of a patient's room in an insane asylum.'

"Could we with ink the ocean fill,

And were the skies of parchment made.

And every stalk on Earth a quill,

And every man a scribe by trade;

To write the love of God above

Would drain the ocean dry;

Nor could the scroll contain the whole

Though stretched from sky to sky."

'So don't feel so sorry for yourself all the time, Lee, for there will always be somebody worse off, and remember what the Roman Centurion said on his return from the Gallic Wars. – "I returned and saw that the race did not go to the swift, nor the battle to the brave, nor bread to the wise man but that time and chance entereth all things".'

Lee felt that for him personally, this would make a fitting epitaph, but having digested a lot of what the old boy said, it made more sense than anything he had ever heard before.

'Lee, I would like to tell you why I gave up everything, and joined this place many years ago. When I was about your age, many years ago, my family owned a small merchant bank in the City of London. I had great prospects and one day my father entrusted me to deliver a package to a Hatton Garden Jewellers. This contained one hundred Krugerrand coins, which are internationally recognised gold bullion. They were difficult to obtain at that time, because of South Africa's apartheid policies, but the jeweller wished to give one to each of his special customers as a Christmas gift. I ordered a taxi to get to the three o'clock appointment on time, but although I arrived on time I was kept waiting until the premises closed. When the manager came and checked the coins he never apologised for the delay, but offered me one of the coins, saying, - "There you go, my boy, take this for your trouble." He dismissed me with a wave of his hand, but I went over and handed the coin back to him saying, "I'm sorry, but that's not the way we do business." That was the first time I realised some people believe money can buy anything, but I never forgot the incident.

Not long afterwards, we got a home visit from a family friend, who had been a missionary in the isolated African country of Rhodesia. Twelve of his comrades stationed in the Elim mission station, up in the Vumba Mountains, had been brutally massacred by twenty-one Mozambique guerrillas who came over the border and attacked everyone with axes and machetes.

Those missionaries were doctors, nurses and ministers who sacrificed their lives to help others living in poverty. One of them, a Mrs. Joyce Lynn, had just opened four health clinics while her husband travelled about the country helping the native people. She had just given birth but, as she clutched the three-week old child in her arms, they were both slaughtered by those merciless butchers. When my friend showed me a photograph of her burned body, I thought she was clutching a small ball in her hand, but she was not. It was her tiny new-born baby, Pamela Grace!

My friend had brought with him a tape cassette, which had been left on during the incident and we heard those missionaries begging God to forgive the guerrillas, as they were in the process of slaughtering them all.

After the war ended, eight of the terrorists, who were in that platoon of butchers, were together in an army camp in Entumbane, over the border, when they experienced visions of Christ crucified, and the hand of God coming against them in judgement.

Seven of them, who had passports, immediately fled the country, but years later enrolled in Bible schools, eventually becoming missionaries themselves! The other, who had no passport, went to Harare and it was there where he also enrolled. He had joined ZANLA, the Zimbabwe African National Liberation Army, which was Robert Mugabe's military wing, at the age of fourteen and was their youngest platoon commander ever, acquiring a devilish reputation, even operating under the nickname of 'War Devil'.

In another later incident a pastor in Harare was preaching when a paraplegic man screamed out in agony for mercy. He confessed he had also been one of those who killed the missionaries, and then testified how those people had prayed for their killers even as they were being slaughtered.

I became bitter and cynical, for I found that although the war there had ceased in order to celebrate Christmas, once the festive season had passed everyone reverted to cruel indifference. For many years this took away any joy of Christmas for me.

Even though Roman Catholic, American Baptist, and Salvation Army clergy had since been slaughtered there, my friend decided to return to those mission-fields. He wrote and explained something amazing to me. He told me how miraculous Christmas was, if people at war could live in harmony and forgiveness with each other for even a few days a year. I suddenly saw that God could redeem the evilest of men, and convert them into the best. This, I realised, was the real miracle so I decided to contribute something to the world myself, as I passed through it on my way to eternity.

What you must realise, Lee, is that it does not matter what wrongs you have done in life, for God came to Earth for sinners which, as mere mortals, we all are. Surely if He forgave those terrorists he can forgive you, and will forgive you, for whatever wrongs you have done if you only repent.

But even if you find faith, my son, and turn to God, have you the courage to forgive yourself? I asked my friend that same Christmas why he still believed in God, and he told me one reason was because in that country he had seen the devil incarnate.'

The old monk then asked Lee, 'Did you tell your friend that you really loved her, when you worked together, or were you too proud?'

'Umm … no.' Lee said quietly, 'I was timid - and just too shy - at the time.'

'Well, I do understand,' ... said his mentor. 'I once met Mother Teresa, who told me that so many people suffer from shyness in this world that it causes as much agony as torture.'

'I'm afraid that may be true,' Lee agreed. 'I think it's a form of self-harm!'

'Remember, Lee what Shakespeare said, ... "It is better to have loved and lost, than never to have loved at all".'

'I would have thought,' said Lee, ... 'surely someone would realise - without the shadow of a doubt, if another person really loved them?'

'Well, ... actually ... no! It's a common fallacy, Lee, for people to assume that because we love them, they will automatically love us in return. Nothing could be further from the truth! Our objects of affection are not typically psychic or gifted with supernatural knowledge. Saying or doing nothing, by deciding your devotion will simply radiate and saturate the object of your affection, is just fantasy and infatuation. Indeed ... unrequited love is possibly the most devastating predicament to be in, and, - unless you can blame some third party for your loss, - you can drive yourself crazy with guilt.'

His mentor continued, 'Lee, I must tell you, ... never be afraid to release your grief through weeping. Bottling up emotions causes hormones to build up in your brain, leaving you constantly depressed. I know that you don't realise it at the moment, but I should tell you all human love is purely temporal, so subject to change. Indeed, there is only one love, which you can always depend on; one that will outlive you and your spouse: - God's love!

And, ... whether you accept or reject it, ... it will remain with you, - up to, and after the moment you die, – for that love alone survives all eternity!'

The old boy concluded, telling Lee, 'It is now midnight, so I must bid you goodnight, for as you know, we all get up at four-thirty ... to pray!'

Lee spent a few more days in the monastery, but he was anxious to return and start afresh. He felt spiritually regenerated and had found new respect for himself and his world, and all the creatures with which he shared it. When the old monk had last spoken to Lee, he told him, 'Just remember it does not matter how or where you met your lost love, or how you felt, or what you did or didn't do; just realise that you once felt pure unconditional love, for another, which is something few of us feel as we wander through life.'

He enjoyed the trip back home, but couldn't wait to charge his phone and find out what had happened to Lucy, whom he now felt was perhaps his last chance at real happiness. He had decided he could not survive alone, and needed a lifelong companion.

He rang Tom for the latest gossip but was totally devastated when he heard that Lucy had hanged herself in her jail cell.

Once again dark clouds of depression swallowed him up like the night. He suddenly remembered the old monk's valedictory blessing. 'Vaya con Dios, my son. Do not let your memories destroy you.'

CHAPTER THIRTEEN

Lee went into another state of depression. He couldn't seem to get to sleep, even with tablets. When he eventually did, he couldn't seem to get out of bed, when he awoke the next day. The doctor advised him to find some goal in his life, which seemed to be aimless at the moment. She suggested he take driving lessons. This fitted in with Lee's plans for he needed to get a licence to drive the sabbers around, as their driver had fled the country. He now realised how fortunate it was that he had never been stopped on his moped, while working in London for the restaurant, or pulled over while driving Ping's car, on the motorway to Hastings. He decided to apply for an intensive full time driving course, for he could now easily afford the one-thousand-pounds' expense involved.

He always knew he would need to reserve money for his return to China but now he could afford to purchase a car, if he passed his test. The intensive two-week course was run from a cheap travel-lodge, and involved a personal instructor, who supervised one lesson every morning, with another after lunch, each of three hours' duration. He would stay at the motel, and study the handbook for the written examination, in the evenings.

The firm declared that they had quick access to all tests by booking in advance, and that their clients rarely failed. If they did, they were given a full refund, or the opportunity of another free course.

Lee decided that, as a full-time commitment it would certainly take his mind off everything, as he would have to concentrate on the course curriculum. He booked in for the following week.

The motel complex was not too far away, and he reached it by bus in forty minutes. There were three qualified instructors available but only two pupils; Lee and one young lady who had already failed the test ten times.

The proprietor explained that this was a quiet time for the school, as the weather was miserable, but their cars were modern and fully equipped. Lee had chosen an automatic, as it was easier and quicker to learn than a manual. The girl opted for a manual car because she had spent most of her time and money on conquering the gearbox technique, with little success.

The first day was given over to studying the Highway Code, and they were each presented with a large 'United Kingdom Driving Manual', for bedtime reading.

'If you learn everything in that book, we'll give you a job here,' laughed the manager.

The next day was spent getting to know the car and its controls. Lee's instructor was bemused when he discovered his pupil's lack of knowledge, but soon decided Lee could be a successful candidate.

The girl fell out of favour when she broke the indicator stalk on the steering wheel by grasping it, instead of merely flicking it on and off. She was informed that this lever controlled not just the indicators but also the lights and the washers, and was very expensive to replace. She did not make another mistake with the hand controls, but later both pupils made bad errors with the foot pedals.

After being tested in the Highway Code it was agreed that the novices would be let loose in traffic the next day. The most important thing with automatics, Lee was told, was to use only one foot at a time. He was asked repeatedly which pedal was for the 'gas', as the accelerator was called, and which pedal was the brake. The first lesson had just been driving around the large car park, where they even practised slow reversing. Lee was then taken the following day to a wide country road, where the instructor switched places and gave him the keys. He stalled on his first attempt, but got over his nervousness and was soon bowling along at nearly thirty miles per hour. The instructor had dual-controls on his side of the car, which was festooned with extra mirrors, one focusing directly on Lee's eyes.

'Ah, you never checked your mirror, before you turned,' he told Lee. 'Remember, M-S-M ... mirror, signal, manoeuvre.' This was not Lee's big mistake. That came later, when they approached a crossroads.

'Note the inverted triangle at the junction with the solid white line. You can ease across split lines, but what must we do here?'

'We must stop,' replied Lee.

'So we ease off the gas, and we press the brake. You don't need to use the handbrake when you stop; once the road is clear just ease up on the foot-brake and press the *gas* pedal ... when you're ready to continue across the junction.'

Lee had been driving all day and was tired, and so was the instructor, but Lee pressed the gas pedal just as they reached the junction, instead of pressing the brake. Before the instructor could react they were shooting straight over the junction. Cars sped by just in front, and even behind them, before they reached the safety of the other side. The instructor was visibly upset.

The girl didn't do so well either. The manager announced that he had to let her go! Over drinks in the lounge that evening the group were told what had happened that afternoon.

Her instructor explained. 'We were driving down the dual carriageway right in the middle of the rush hour. I decided we should turn right up a side street, to escape the traffic. She had pulled up in a gap of the central reservation, leading off the dual carriageway, and we were waiting to enter the side road on our right.

Waiting alongside us, for a break in the traffic, was a sports convertible. I was very tired, but relaxed, when I noticed the driver of the other car impatiently revving his engine, looking for a break in the traffic. Lorries and buses were hurtling past, but when this guy suddenly spied a gap in traffic, he revved up and shot straight over, leaving us behind in a cloud of smoke.

But our girl decides, if he can do it - so can I. So she revs up and tries to follow him across, lifting the clutch too sharply and making the bloody car stall.

The trouble is, we have actually stalled halfway across the road, blocking the traffic, and here is this juggernaut thundering towards us. I see the driver's face freeze in horror, so I grabs me door handle to jump out. Suddenly I have flashing visions of the Press headlines … "Instructor Abandons Pupil to Die" and "Driving School Closes Down."

Anyway, our car is still in first gear, but she's frozen in fear, so I leans over and twists the ignition key so the starter motor could jerk us across the rest of the road. We just made it, for that juggernaut had started to jack-knife.'

The next day the girl was conspicuous by her absence. She had passed her written test, as had Lee, so it was a shame and a waste of effort, although she was given a full refund.

Lee persevered and took his test nine days later. He had driven many hours in that particular car, but there was a last minute panic when he was told there was a problem with his car, for someone had booked it in for a service that day and he would have to use another one. Lee started to panic for he couldn't get used to the controls of the new car, as the indicators were on a different side of the steering wheel, and he found that the seat had been soaked by perspiration, from a previous candidate who had just failed. This car had been borrowed from another branch of the school, but Lee insisted they supply him the car that he was accustomed to, for his test; they did so at the very last minute, which calmed him down. He relaxed, and sailed through the test with just one minor fault, of stalling on a hill-start.

When he drove back to the centre with his pass-slip the instructor declared, 'I knew you'd passed as soon as you drove into the car park. One gets an instinct for these things, and even when I'm waiting back at the driving centre I can sense if my pupil has failed or not, even before they return.'

Lee managed to get the last bus home to Hastings, after he had bought the instructor a few drinks and paid the bill for his motel. It had been an expensive business, he considered, but well worth it.

Tom had connections with the motor trade and could advise him on what sort of car he could afford, but on his return to Hastings memories of Lucy came flooding back, and in the mailbox he found an invitation to her cremation service, which had been delayed so that an autopsy could be conducted.

It was a wet windy morning that found Lee and a small group of friends, greeting each other in the spacious room opposite the crematorium chapel. Lucy had no parents and few friends so it was a very sad occasion. They filed into the chapel where her sealed coffin lay on the altar next to a high wall adorned with full-length purple curtains. There were tributes and floral bouquets and even a wreath, which were all placed outside in the annex.

As the service started everyone rose to sing 'Amazing Grace', which really moved Lee as he had never heard it before.

A minister presided, preaching that, ... 'We all come into the world naked, and we all leave naked; for dust we are and unto dust we shall return. If we live a righteous life we leave something behind and someone to remember us, but man who is born of woman is full of misery, and has but a short time to live.'

This dismal message drew out a few handkerchiefs, and even Lee felt choked.

The music was simple and after a eulogy was delivered by one of her friends, the song 'My Way' was played over the speakers, as the purple curtains parted and the coffin was drawn slowly away, to where the ovens were waiting.

Afterwards, there was an informal wake in the Railway Tavern, a favourite haunt of the sabbers, where sandwiches and snacks were provided. Everyone agreed they had just buried a martyr but her death would not be in vain.

There were a few people indulging in cannabis, but no mushrooms were produced. Lee was extolling their virtues to the crowd, when someone took offence and tackled him. Apparently this guy had a girlfriend who had experienced a bad trip, and had been locked up in a secure ward for years, just smiling at the walls all day. This stranger resented anybody encouraging the use of drugs, so Lee decided to make an exit before drink got the better of him.

He needed to speak to Tom, but as he walked home he reflected that alcohol was also a drug, and that had caused much more damage to society than toxic mushrooms.

Lee rang Tom, who informed him he had a number of cars, which might be of interest to him, ranging from a little Mini Cooper to an old but fast Mitsubishi GTO, which 'looked the business' but would be expensive to maintain. Next day Tom picked Lee up, and they drove from Hastings to a place in the country where his friend had a garage. There, it was explained that all the cars for sale were taken in part exchange and apart from having a current MOT certificate of roadworthiness, carried no guarantee. The Mini felt too cramped for Lee but he fell in love with the GTO. It was a twin-turbo three-litre, which had been specially 'chipped' for acceleration rather than top speed, but would still do about one hundred and fifty miles-per-hour.

Lee sensed he might need a fast car in the near future, as things seemed to be catching up with him, and a fast getaway could prove useful. He loved the shape and the colour of the 'beast' and was delighted to learn that not only had it four-wheel drive but also possessed four-wheel steering.

They bartered the price down to five thousand pounds, twice that of the Mini, and Lee was taken for a drive.

'How many miles on it?' enquired Lee.

'How many do you want?' laughed the dealer.

'This thing is over twenty years old, but only has seventy-five-thousand genuine miles on the clock,' declared the dealer, 'and I've got the paperwork to prove it. It's a twin-turbo, and will do sixty in less than six seconds. It goes like shit off a shovel, but will cost you an arm and a leg in petrol because the last owner got it 'chipped' for speed rather than economy. It will only do about twelve to the gallon, but if you keep it under fifty mile-an-hour you might get twenty.'

Lee had no intention of keeping it under fifty, or under a hundred, come to that!

He was hooked in seconds when the beast leapt off the line to a squeal of tyres and the smell of burning rubber as they shot off down the road.

'They only made automatics in this model, with simple paddle switches, - for really fast gear-changes, mounted directly on the steering-wheel; these allow you to keep pace with a fast-revving engine,' explained the dealer.

As Lee declared his undying love for the car he was informed by the dealer that it would need a new set of rear wheel bearings in the near future and a new set of back pipes. He then added, 'The standard ones are usually stainless steel, and cost over a grand, but I know where you can get them made up for a few hundred.'

For a second-hand car dealer, Lee was surprised at the man's frankness, as he also told him how to obtain cheap insurance, claiming the vehicle, now over twenty years old, could be insured as a Classic car.

Lee travelled home, after thanking Tom for all his help and advice. He contacted an insurance company, who agreed to insure him, after learning that he had held a Chinese licence for many years.

Lee promptly decided he could now afford the car of his dreams. He knew the insurance company had no way of verifying his details in China, as Ping had given him an old Chinese licence which he'd used for years in London. He wasn't worried, as he had been economical with the truth on some other points, which he fully realised would invalidate any future claims. He had neglected to mention some relevant facts, like the car would not actually be garaged overnight, and that he might possibly exceed the mileage limit placed on 'classic' cars.

The next day Lee returned, paid cash, and collected the car. Tom drove it back to Hastings at a leisurely pace. It was decided the best place to park up would be the seafront, as this vehicle was too conspicuous to steal, being one of a kind in the whole county of Sussex.

Tom then collected his own car and Lee thanked him sincerely for all his help. When Tom had gone Lee returned to the car and went for a drive. He put a few gallons of fuel in at the nearest garage and took the car for a spin, ending up in Newhaven.

It took him a while to get used to the cornering technique required with four-wheel steering, but he found it was almost impossible to lose control around a bend. The acceleration was breath-taking, and he was often pushed back in the seat, like taking-off in a plane.

In Newhaven he spotted a group of lads revving up cars in an abandoned car park, and stopped nearby. One sauntered over to admire his car, and then called his mates over. They were all enthusiasts, who had 'pimped' their cars, and spent fortunes tuning them. As Lee inspected their Subarus and Mitsubishis he noticed one driver even had an old Nissan Skyline, an original 'muscle-car'.

He asked the owner how expensive it was, and he replied. 'It cost me forty-thousand pounds, but I've put another ten into it, so it stands me fifty grand, if you want to buy it?'

'What! ...' said Lee ruefully, 'I could just afford five, for my GTO. Got it cheap, as it's twenty years old, but it's classed as a classic.' The Skyline owner was not impressed, telling Lee his insurance cost him more than that, and walked off, leaving Lee gazing at the exotic paint and pristine condition of a Toyota Supra; another sort of cheap supercar.

Another collector's item caught his attention. It was a Jaguar 'S' type, but not the normal six cylinder three litre version, but a Type 'R', which has an eight cylinder supercharged engine of over four litres. These produce over four hundred horsepower, and Lee figured it was among the fastest vehicles present. He chatted to the owner who told him he found it on the internet for ten grand, and figured it was a real bargain.

All the owners kept their engines in spotless condition, with everything polished and chromed, and most had colourful new wiring harnesses installed. Even the underneath of their cars sported coloured lighting.

They challenged Lee to a race back to Lewes, on the road they seemed to use as a kind of private test track; but he declined.

He explained he had only just bought the car and wasn't used to it; besides, he didn't want to wreck it on his first day out. They promised to meet up again, explaining that there was always a crowd gathered at that particular spot by the railway station, on Friday and Saturday nights. Lee later discovered that they all raced to the Lewes roundabout every weekend, when huge sums of money changed hands. He decided he could do with some of that, so resolved to acquire expertise with his new car, as he realised it was just as fast as any of the souped-up vehicles the others possessed.

In the days to come Lee was a frequent visitor to Newhaven, where the gang showed him how to execute handbrake-turns and reverse-spins. When they agreed he was ready, they voted him into the club, presenting him with the gift of a shiny rotating knob, which clamped onto his steering wheel giving him the ability to turn the steering faster than normal. Now he was accepted as one of them; one of the Newhaven 'crew'.

CHAPTER FOURTEEN

Lee still visited the park café to keep in contact with the saboteurs. Through them he heard about an upcoming fashion event in Brighton, where all the models would be sporting fur coats. It was 'Venus in Furs' week, and the major fashion-houses' *avant-garde* would all be in attendance.

The thing that seemed to incense the saboteurs most, was the fact that one of the most famous models in the world who had insured her legs for a million pounds, had declared she would wear the most expensive coat on offer. This particular coat had been especially made for her, from the rare pelts of wild Siberian wolves.

Lucy told Lee that wild bears are also hunted in Siberia by rich foreigners, who pay handsomely for a camouflaged hide to be set up, with all the comforts of home. The hide is positioned opposite some remote cave, where a mother bear has given birth over the winter. As she sleepily emerges after hibernation, leaving her cubs inside the cave while she starts to forage, the hunters shoot and kill her. The cubs, blind for a month, then starve to death, because if the bear does escape, her sense of self-preservation prevents her returning to the cave.

Lee learned that this famous model had been feted by 'PETA', the animal rights movement, years earlier, for her refusal to wear fur of any kind. That was a time when people followed women down the street, if they were wearing fur coats, and sprayed them with red dye.

'These days there is absolutely no need to kill animals for their fur,' declared Lucy.

'So tell me,' said Lee, 'what about all those bearskin hats, which I spotted outside Buckingham Palace?'

'The guardsmen say those things generate more respect, and snap-shots of course, from the general public,' said Lucy, 'but I still think the bearskin looks better on the bear. Currently, there are regiments in eight countries who support this atrocity. Mostly the fashion of Grenadier Guardsmen, who in years gone by needed hats without brims, because any brim could hinder their throwing of grenades. So busbies, and then brimless bearskins were adopted, which had the bonus of making the soldiers look taller and more imposing; sadly, this tradition continues, despite worldwide condemnation.'

The group in the café were determined to protest but worried for their safety, for they thought Lucy had been 'disposed of' by the authorities claiming she would never hang herself. They were scared of being seen anywhere near the huge exhibition hall where the venue would be held, although Lee offered to give them a lift to the event.

Lee listened carefully. Then he quietly told them not to protest at the venue, promising to fix things so that nothing similar would ever happen again. He didn't go into any details but did tell them that he would expose this blatant hypocrisy to the whole world.

Everyone was sworn to secrecy, and Lee left the café with their words of support, ringing in his ears.

He now felt committed so planned his next move. He saw that the affair was billed as a charity event and anyone could buy a ticket for five hundred pounds. This was going to deplete his savings but he drew cash out and went to a tour operator to purchase a ticket. After a brief phone call from the agent, he was pleased to learn he had managed to secure one of the last tickets available.

Some days before the event, he made a point of driving to Brighton to spy out the venue. He gained entry to the auditorium, inside the hotel complex, by producing an old business card of Pings and claiming his firm had been offered the contract to supply the hors d'oeuvres and other snacks for the event. Lee was impressed, gazing at the huge chandeliers and subtle hidden lighting around the catwalk. The stage was set and all the guest tables were in place, surrounding the catwalk.

He walked around the hall, admiring the elaborate curtains draped around the catwalk and noted that there seemed to be lots of space underneath. He then inquired where the food trolleys would be kept during the performance, and was informed that the organisers had decided that the best place would be under the catwalk itself, to avoid pilfering. This suited Lee's purpose perfectly.

A gang of workmen were erecting a huge wire antenna round the whole area, which would transmit a radio commentary of the proceedings to those in the audience wearing hearing aids. He knew this was normal practice as modern hearing aids have a switch for such occasions.

Lee then drove back to Hastings, and sat down to plan his next move. He lay awake in bed, for most of the night, but by morning had devised a plan of action.

The venue was in the exhibition hall adjacent to the seafront and part of a large hotel complex.

He would contrive a bomb scare to stop the proceedings taking place. This would have to be a viable device that the authorities could not simply ignore. It had to constitute a real threat to the proceedings.

He would telephone a warning, early the next day, so that the premises could be searched and the bomb discovered. He would bluff that there was more than one device installed so they would have to cancel the show, if they couldn't find the other one, which of course they wouldn't, for he planned to leave just a single device.

He would use the drone Tom had lent him, to monitor the comings and goings of the emergency services, once he had armed the device from the safety of the nearby seafront and telephoned a warning.

Lee felt this was a brilliant idea, as he could relax on the beach and stay as long as required, to confirm his device had been discovered and the show cancelled.

He started by visiting a theatrical supplier who sold him a 'stage maroon'. These are normally used in pantomimes for creating the effect of a sudden explosion of smoke and are detonated by a small battery.

He then purchased a small quantity of fireworks, and a couple of cheap mobile phones from a supermarket for which he paid cash. The final items needed were obtained from a pharmacist, and were small plastic containers of butane gas, used for heating curling tongs. He already had a supply of liquid 'Cold-Packs', which had been prescribed for his back pain, and was aware that these were filled with a form of ammonium nitrate, a common explosive used in quarry-blasting. He extracted the spent carbon-dioxide gas cylinder from his soda siphon, and sawed the nozzle off, at the top. He had picked up some tips from Ping back in London, who had on occasion firebombed rival premises.

Ping simply used match-heads, which Lee had cut off to construct his models, but Ping put them to good use. He would drop a few hundred into a paper cone, used by take-away restaurants for french-fries, and place this into the spout of a large plastic container of petrol. After positioning the device, he would carefully balance a thin candle into the middle of the match heads. When he was confident that the candle was stable he would light it, and retreat. In the short time the candle took to burn down, igniting the match-heads, he would have made good his escape. As the match-heads burnt through the paper cone, some of them would drop into the container, which would then flare up and melt, causing the place to be swamped with burning petrol. Within minutes the container and all the evidence would be consumed in the inferno.

Lee started to construct his own device, wearing thin gloves, to avoid leaving any DNA.

Ping had also taught him how to construct the simple but deadly bomb he was now ready to build. Firstly, he stripped the casing from the stage-maroon, and carefully extracted the tiny capsule of mercury-fulminate, commonly used to ignite these devices. It was a tiny red blob with two wires protruding. When connected to a battery it would explode, igniting the powder in the maroon.

The next job was to open up the two phones so that their speaker wires could be disconnected. He wired the first set of speaker wires so that the ring-tone voltage of this phone would switch on the other phone, priming the device for detonation. Then, if the second phone was rung its speaker voltage would activate the capsule of mercury fulminate and the bomb would explode.

He inserted the capsule inside the metal carbon dioxide soda cylinder. Then breaking open the fireworks he collected a small amount of gunpowder, which he sieved into the empty cylinder around the capsule.

He sealed the opening with epoxy-resin and now had his detonator. Ping had taught him that gunpowder was a 'low' explosive, whereas the flaky powders from shotgun-cartridges and bullets were nitro-cellulose, and just propellants. Ping boasted that the Chinese were using gunpowder when the West was running round with bows and arrows.

'Low' explosives were needed to ignite 'high' explosives like C4 or even R.D.X., but Lee knew he wouldn't need any of those, as his sole intention was just to get the show cancelled and scare these people into rethinking their ambition to reverse the current slump in the fur market. He just wanted an incendiary device and proceeded to construct one, by surrounding the detonator with the plastic butane-gas cylinders, which he then covered with his Cold-Packs. He used plastic garden-ties, to clamp these around the detonator.

The mercury fulminate would ignite the gunpowder which itself would force the butane gas into the ammonium nitrate, vaporising it, and causing spontaneous combustion, which it would only do when it acquired enough oxygen from the surrounding air. This is known, *in the trade,* as a Fuel-Air bomb.

Lee checked the wiring and the phones before he packed the device inside a large loaf of bread, which he had hollowed out; he then resealed it, in its plastic packet. This innocuous package, waiting to be served as snacks after the show, could be left on the food trolleys beneath the catwalk ... nobody would think twice about a loaf of bread on a food trolley.

But when Lee retired that night he didn't sleep for he realised if his plan backfired, and the bomb did explode, it would ignite the whole interior and torch the catwalk completely.

Bright and early the next morning, to avoid the bottleneck on the Brighton road, he set of in his GTO.

He arrived earlier than expected so took the time to park in an all-day underground car park.

He was amongst the first to gain entry with his ticket, but had to wait in the foyer until the exhibition doors were opened. While he waited, he sat in the lounge with a cup of coffee, cradling the loaf-bomb in his lap.

Shortly afterwards, the hotel porters opened the large double-doors, and he watched them walk across to the coffee machine. Lee observed some hotel maids placing food trolleys nearby, and assumed they could only be for the venue, so he casually sauntered over and placed his loaf-bomb on the bottom shelf of a trolley. He made sure he avoided the video camera, which he had spotted on his earlier visit, but realised he was still taking a chance.

The porters soon returned with their coffees, and casually watched as the two food trolleys were stacked with an assortment of snacks, leaving his loaf in place. He was greatly relieved when the maids proceeded to wheel the food trolleys into the hall, putting them under the catwalk, where the drapes covered them completely. As Lee was leaving the hotel, a security van pulled up outside. He paused to watch as a couple of guards carried an ornate box into the hall. A small crowd had gathered, and people were taking snapshots on their phones. Lee asked someone what all the fuss was about. He learned that one of the models would be wearing a bespoke item of jewellery. Apparently this was a fur bikini costume encrusted with diamonds, worth over a million dollars, which had been pictured in all the morning newspapers.

Lee was shocked that he hadn't noticed any publicity over this garment, which Mona Cambele would display under her wolf-skin fur coat ... worth a fortune in itself.

The guards who delivered the item looked like they were settling in for the duration, because they took up positions inside the exhibition complex.

Lee retired to the beach, which the hotel overlooked, and started playing around with the tiny drone that Tom had lent him. It was only a couple of inches long and when it flew up in the air nobody noticed the noise above the din of the traffic. Although the weather was gusty, his previous experience of flying kites gave Lee full control of the gadget, even in difficult conditions.

He had practised at home with the device and was fairly competent, but made sure he had charged the batteries of both the drone and the mobile phones. He had logged their numbers into his own mobile and made sure he knew which one to ring first, to arm his device. He retrieved the drone and waited until a queue built up outside the centre. There was a brief commotion as some of the models arrived, and were asked to pose for a herd of photographers, before being escorted into the VIP lounge.

Lee knew the performance was not scheduled for another hour, but of course everybody had to get ready and change into costumes. Apparently, they would all wear swimwear beneath their fur coats, and the whole ensemble promised to be a truly glamourous affair.

The proceedings were not due to start until midday, but everybody expected the usual delays. Nevertheless,

Lee rang the police early, on a separate phone which he had never used before.

He fed his voice through a novelty toy; a device used to change peoples' voices. On the gadget, he selected the option for a Donald Duck accent and told the operator in New Scotland Yard that there were a number of bombs planted in the exhibition hall as a protest against fur-farming.

It wasn't long before he heard lots of sirens as the bomb squad arrived. On his drone camera he was able to observe as two chaps, dressed in huge cumbersome suits and helmets, lumbered into the hall.

At least they were taking things seriously. Fire alarms had been activated in the hotel and the staff had fled, leaving the background music blaring away. Lee could even hear it from the beach nearby. To ensure that they would find his loaf-bomb he immediately rang the first phone, which of course, also armed the device. This should be easily discovered, as he had checked that it could be clearly heard although it was buried in the bread.

Unfortunately, it wasn't heard, because the background music obliterated its ring tone. Lee was confident they would discover it sooner or later, so he kept it ringing but the loud music was still playing and the phone battery ran out of power, although it had already primed the bomb. Lee now realised that if anyone rang the second number the device would instantly detonate, for he had no way of disarming it; but he was still relaxed, because nobody could have the specific eleven-digit number required for the second phone and the odds of someone accidentally ringing it were beyond astronomical.

He watched through his drone camera as the bomb squad declared a false alarm, and made their exit an hour later. The security guards were now on their toes for they suspected some attempt was being made to capture the precious jewelled bikini, currently secured in the hotel safe, but nobody really knew what was happening. Lee realised the show would still go ahead, but all was not lost, because he knew the bomb would later be discovered when someone found the loaf, which should not be there with the hors d'oeuvres. The bomb would be safe unless the second phone received a signal, but reports of his device would soon leak out, and the catwalk models would all think twice about any further exploitation of animals, after such a narrow escape.

The show was about to start; there was nothing more that Lee could do, so he started packing his drone up, and took the SIM card out of his phone before chucking it in the sea. Just before he got up to leave the beach, a flash of intense light hit him, followed by a blast and the sound of an enormous explosion. He only discovered later what had happened.

The lengthy enquiry, which followed, concluded that the antenna used to transmit a commentary to all the hearing aids had generated a signal sufficient to activate any mobile phones inside the perimeter.

The organisers were aware of this, for they had asked everyone to switch off their phones before the show began, but Lee didn't have that information.

When the applause for the entrance of Mona Cambele had subsided, the announcer, who had just started to expound on the virtues of her jewelled costume, had only begun to speak before the whole auditorium was engulfed in a fireball.

Blame for the massive loss of life was laid on the security guards, who had immediately locked all the exits when they heard the explosion, preventing escape. They claimed they panicked, believing a robbery was occurring, because they already had to deal with a false bomb scare in the hall just before the show.

Apparently, the bomb had detonated once it had received a radio-pulse from the antenna and then spread the butane gas around the room, which combusted when it surrounded the *fashionista,* and the star of the show, who was incinerated in her beautiful fur coat, as it burned to a crisp.

It was later acknowledged that the diamond costume didn't help, because the diamonds had combusted with the intense heat. Most people do not realise that diamonds, being formed from carbon, ignite if exposed to over seven hundred degrees centigrade.

The authorities estimated that the fireball, which killed so many, was nearly two thousand degrees, for butane gas burns at that temperature. Consequently, no efforts were made in the autopsy, to retrieve any remnant of diamond from Ms. Cambele's remains!

Lee left the scene before it was cordoned off and had to go for a stiff drink before he was able to retrieve his car and drive slowly home. When he reached the safety of his flat he took an overdose of sleeping tablets and went to bed, not caring if he never … ever, woke up again.

CHAPTER FIFTEEN

Two days later Lee did wake up; he didn't really want to, but a raging thirst and a splitting headache dragged him back to reality.

Over a breakfast of strong coffee, he did a lot of hard thinking. He was now responsible for many lives, but the irony was that he never set out to take a single one. Things had simply not turned out the way he intended, but he still felt guilty and ashamed and decided he must change everything; his lifestyle: his home, and his friends.

He decided he must return to China, but now had little money left, for he had recently put new twenty-inch wheels, and low-profile tyres on the GTO and these had cost him an extra two thousand pounds.

Still, he had a few thousand left, but not enough to buy him safe passage to China and start afresh, so he considered a last-ditch option for acquiring the funds he needed. The crew at the car club in Newhaven were organising their annual event. This was a race for high stakes and even bookies got involved in the proceedings, for the prize money was twenty-five thousand pounds.

He sobered up enough to motor over to the car park and enter the race. The entry fee was a thousand pounds, and he bet another thousand on himself. The crew had worked his odds out at ten to one, so if he did happen to win he would collect thirty-five thousand in total, which would grant him the lifestyle he wanted in the 'old country'.

The race was to take place over the usual circuit by the Lewes roundabout, except this time it was not just a race there and a cruise back; the winner was the first one to return to the car park in Newhaven.

Saturday night arrived, and a horde of cars and supporters had gathered at the venue. There were a lot of drink and drugs floating about, but Lee abstained, for he knew this was his do-or-die moment. The partying went on until the early hours, for the race was not scheduled until three in the morning when the roads would be deathly quiet.

He was going to gamble his life as he reckoned he was living on borrowed time anyway, and had nothing to lose in a last-ditch effort to redeem himself and escape from the country that had given him so much grief.

All the cars and drivers were spruced up and lots of photos were taken, with lots of pretty girls, posing with lots of drivers. Most of the drivers were younger than Lee and he realised they had more experience. He hoped his reflexes might be just as fast, but his intention was not merely to stay alive; it was to win the prize money. He didn't care much if the road took him, for at least it would be quicker than rotting in a jail cell for the rest of his life.

He recalled being locked up with Ping beside men who knew they would never be released. He recalled how those men would howl the night away in anguish and despair.

There were twenty cars in the race and they would all set off in a straight line. Lee noticed some of the more expensive models had been withdrawn at the last minute, as the owners treasured their vehicles too much to lose them in a stupid race. These toys were their pride and joy and sometimes all they owned, or could afford.

They spent all their time and money tuning them to perfection and were not going to risk everything if they were not totally confident they could win the race. In fact, every one of the drivers who did enter the race was convinced that they alone would collect the prize-money and the status that night. They never considered they might lose their lives as well as their cars.

A pretty girl hoisted a white flag in full view of the car park. There was a gap of a hundred yards before the dual carriageway, and the first cars to reach it stood the best chance of winning. Lee's car was very fast on take-off, but he noticed the Toyota Supra was on his left, while the Nissan Skyline was placed to his right. This car was a twin-turbo three-litre similar to Lee's but produced nearly five hundred horsepower at six-thousand-eight-hundred revs. His own car was only about four hundred horsepower, but was chipped for acceleration rather than top speed. Lee felt this was an advantage for nobody could go over a hundred and fifty on these winding roads.

What the other drivers didn't know, and what Lee didn't tell them, was that earlier that week he had parked at the Lewes roundabout and walked the five miles into Newhaven and back. His idea was to know the course perfectly, sizing up which corners had bad 'camber' and at what speeds he could safely enter them; what line to take, where to brake and where to accelerate.

He did this for every bend and it took him all day. He even sat down by the long curving dip, near Newhaven, which was approached by a bend and exited by a blind corner. He figured this dangerous spot might be used to advantage by a desperate driver if he was prepared to exit that final bend on the wrong side of the road.

The following night, he practised on the road at that very spot. He waited until the last ferries from France had driven past to their destinations in England before attempting this manoeuvre, because he knew that sometimes a sleepy continental driver would automatically drive on the right side of the road here, because he had been accustomed to driving on the right, before boarding the ferry.

Consequently, large signs were erected at the harbour exit, to warn continental drivers that they now had to change lanes and drive on the left.

He drove the road a few times, getting faster and more confident each and every time. These particular bends suited his four wheel steering as long as he kept the power on, and he realised he could be the fastest car over that particular spot. He was getting used to the bumpy ride, which his very low-profile tyres exerted on the chassis, but the massive grip they provided compensated for any lack of comfort. He had also fitted a double-belted full seat harness, as the G-force in his car was now capable of tossing him from side to side.

But now the moment everyone was waiting for, arrived. The girl in the short skirt dropped the white flag and Lee thought most of the drivers must have looking at her legs instead of the flag, for he shot off the line first and reached the road just in front of the Nissan Skyline.

He was hitting ninety before he realised that being in the lead had no real advantage, for he was literally lighting the road up for the rest of the pack, and acting as pacemaker. At least the rain had held off and the roads were not too dusty. There was no traffic about at that time on a Sunday morning, as all the ferries had stopped running. Newhaven was the last town at the end of that road, unless you wanted to jump off Beachy Head. With the locals tucked up in bed ready for Monday morning, the crew had the road to themselves, which is why they choose this neck of the woods for their exploits.

Lee rounded the first corner at nearly a hundred, but was now faced with a long stretch of straight road. He could scarcely glance at the speedometer, but kept an eye on the rev-counter mounted directly in front of him. He was annoyed but not surprised when the huge Skyline rushed past him at what he estimated was at least one hundred and fifty miles-per-hour. He relaxed somewhat when a quick glance in the mirror told him the rest of the pack were all well behind.

He couldn't catch the Skyline until the large Lewes roundabout where he cornered ferociously and passed it on the wrong side of the road as they exited, narrowly missing the rest of the pack, approaching the other way.

He didn't keep his lead for more than a mile when another long stretch of straight road enabled the Skyline to fly past like the wind. The thing was so fast he felt that he had little chance of catching up, and lost all hope of winning, but fate intervened.

A Romanian driver at the docks had been discovered with illegal aliens hiding in his refrigerated lorry. He was held up for hours and given a huge fine, so on leaving the port, was so upset that he started driving on the wrong side of the road.

The Skyline driver felt confident of success, realising he was well ahead of Lee and the rest of the field, but on a blind corner had to suddenly run off the road as he encountered this Romanian juggernaut heading straight for him with headlights blazing. He skidded onto the verge and his engine stalled, but he was able to quickly shoot off again, still retaining the lead. However, this occurred near the tricky bends with the steep dip, so Lee now realised this was the one place where he just might regain the lead. He reached the Skyline, which had now re-started and bolted off, just before the spot where he had practised on the double bends the night before.

He lined up the Skyline as he approached the first corner and shot into the bend fast enough to slipstream the black beast. He knew this was his last opportunity so used all his cornering power to manoeuvre to the right of the Skyline. He had now lost the slipstream, but was able to catapult out of the last bend by pressing the gas pedal with his right foot while feathering the brake with his left. As his torque transmission built up latent energy, screaming to change down a gear, he lined up his exit and quickly lifted his left foot off the brake, forcing the gearbox to make a lightning change with a sudden jump in revs. Now the engine fed all its dormant energy into the four-wheel drive, which catapulted him past the Skyline on the wrong side of the road.

He was helped by the distraction of a huge bang behind him, as both of them realised that one of the others had come to grief. The Skyline driver seemed to be in a state of shock, for he never attempted to retake the lead from Lee, knowing he would have to risk everything to get past; so Lee threw his GTO into the Newhaven car park, screeching in ahead of the Skyline, to tumultuous cheering and the blast of car horns.

The crowd couldn't hang around for long, for everyone realised the police and emergency services would soon arrive, as it appeared the young driver of the Jaguar had hit a tree at speed. This was tragic, for a wall or a house or even a truck would have afforded him some chance of survival, but not a tree, for trees do not budge.

Lee was presented with his prize money before the cheering crowd, who showered him with champagne just before everyone jumped in their cars and roared off.

Later that week, they all attended a memorial service for the young man who was still in his teens, but as his girlfriend stated at the service, he died doing what he lived for, which was doing what he did best.

CHAPTER SIXTEEN

In London when Lee was granted a visa for turning state's evidence, he was eligible for long-term residency and that cleared the way for a British passport, for which he now applied.

This took a number of weeks even though he paid for it to be fast-tracked. He wondered if anyone had fingered him for some recent event and waited weeks in trepidation.

He knew there was no DNA, or fingerprint, to link him to anything, for the fires in the barn and the hotel had destroyed all the evidence. For the moment he was a free man, but realised that some of the animal rights people may have guessed he was behind certain incidents, so he waited with bated breath until he received his passport. Officially, Lee was a Chinese citizen, but he couldn't apply in England for a Chinese passport. He scribbled a short letter to La-Lu, saying goodbye and asking her to remember him, as he would shortly be leaving the country for good. He didn't go into details, but told her he hoped to return to China and the village where they had both worked in the dog markets. He confessed that he had done a U-turn, and was now an animal lover, even hoping to change the attitudes of the people in the meat markets when he returned home. In actual fact he planned to burn down the dog markets in the village where he used to work.

Lee dropped off to see Tom and gave him the GTO to look after and told him that, as he might not be coming back, he could do what he wanted with the car, after a year. He had originally planned to ship the car over in a container, which he could easily afford, but remembered that everyone drove on the right in China, so he would be at an immediate disadvantage in a right-hand drive car, and also realised he had no idea what the traffic would be like after his long absence.

Lee figured Tom would be so enamoured with the GTO that, after a year, he would want to keep the car rather than sell it.

He never let any of the café crowd know he was leaving, for he knew just one vindictive phone-call could jeopardise his escape plans. His last act before catching the train to Gatwick airport was to visit the grave of his little dog, where the saboteurs had buried it behind bushes in the park.

He was only permitted to take ten thousand Chinese Yuan, about two thousand English Pounds, into China.

Lee managed to convert the rest of his money into American Dollars, acquiring some five-hundred-dollar notes, which he taped onto each leg. The two packages of forty notes each were inconspicuous under his thick compression stockings, which all the passengers were advised to wear, to avoid potential leg thrombosis on the twelve-hour flight to Beijing.

At Gatwick, Lee checked in his suitcase with his little travel bag and after collecting the boarding pass, relaxed in one of the lounge bars, partaking of a vegetarian hamburger. At customs he had to take his shoes off but thankfully not his socks, and having passed safely through security, bought some light refreshments for the flight. These had to be kept sealed, until he was actually on board the plane, a Boeing 747-400, capable of seating four hundred travellers.

He marvelled at the speed of the take-off. He heard nearby passengers mumbling what he took to be prayers, but he just tried to compare the acceleration of this jet to that of his GTO. He optimistically decided he could beat it up to a hundred miles-an-hour, but the huge four-engine plane had to go faster than one-fifty for take-off, or rotation as it is known, and it also needed at least a thousand metres of runway.

Lee and most of the passengers were now relaxed, because everyone knows the most dangerous time in any flight is take-off. He had heard that these huge planes were especially hazardous, for if an engine caught fire they could not land immediately, as the massive fuel load would create too heavy an impact on the runway and the plane would instantly explode.

He also knew that plane fuel was similar to diesel in as much that it was hard to ignite, unless under pressure, but if it impacted the ground at the landing speed of a jetliner, it would spontaneously combust.

Lee took some tablets in an effort to sleep on the plane, for he wanted to avoid jet-lag after arrival. He had set his watch to central China time and managed to snooze for most of the flight, under the warmth of the blanket supplied by the China Airways attendant. There was a little turbulence, but otherwise the flight was uneventful, and he arrived in Beijing in time to book into a central hotel. He didn't relish paying premium prices, but told himself he could now afford it. He also arranged the long-term lease of a Mercedes SLK convertible, for his long drive to the 'dog-village'.

The following day saw a late start for he slept late and awoke with a headache. He went to the dining room and ate as much as he could, before re-packing his case and heading off on his journey. This car had a modern Sat-Nav built in, so he was able to speak co-ordinates into it and the car directed him onto the easiest route. He was glad to leave the city, for although the buildings were staggeringly beautiful, there were too many people about and Lee detested crowds. He could not help but be impressed by the view, illuminated at night by millions of neon lights, casting myriad glows around the darkening sky.

Lee liked driving at night; it was quieter and you could see oncoming traffic by their headlights, but it still took him five hours to reach his destination. He arrived, too tired to do anything, so simply fell asleep in the car, after folding the seats right back.

The bustle of thousands of early morning commuters, cycling to work, woke Lee from a deep sleep. He decided he had better book in somewhere nice, where he could garage his lovely Mercedes.

In daylight he began to recognise the area, which seemed to have drastically changed, with many new housing structures, built since the Olympics some years back. He found a reasonable Travel Lodge motel where the car could safely be left. He selected a fully serviced room with breakfast available if required. He could afford better, but he wanted to spy out the lie of the land, and his first priority was to visit the market.

He decided to walk, but felt a strange sense of shame overcome him as he heard, as though for the first time, the sounds of birds singing overhead. Of course there had always been birds there, and of course they always sang; it was just that Lee had never noticed the birds, or the trees, or any of the beauty that had surrounded him. The tiny birds gathered in the high branches and twittered harmoniously, while the larger species flocked on nearby telephone wires and squawked at each other.

Before he arrived at the market he also noticed the intermittent howling of the dogs, something his mind had also blanked out, but he let his ears guide him and soon arrived at the sheds where he used to work many years ago.

He was stunned to see his old boss still in action. The old boy recognised Lee immediately and invited him round the back for tea.

'You look prosperous, my boy,' he exclaimed. 'Have the years been kind to you?'

'Well, I'm still alive,' grinned Lee.

'What about you, Chen, have things changed much round here?' he asked.

'Well, after you left new people from Korea took over, and they treat the dogs a lot worse, but I still get a percentage off the market manager if I look after our special customers. And now we also deal with crocodile meat. Every weekend a small truck arrives here, with a large crocodile anchored in the back. When they dump it in the street it's then tied down with ropes, and the customers all run round to mark out their favourite joint, which is then cut from the beast as it's thrashing about. After that I have little trouble hacking off its limbs, although it will still be alive. Changing the subject, I must tell you, that rich Madam Zsa-Zsa, who was your special customer sent her daughter to acting school and now she has appeared in a couple of Kung-Fu movies, so is quite famous around here. Her name is Amy Sang and she really is very beautiful.'

'Don't tell me,' Lee responded, 'I remember her as a precocious teenager.'

As the old man gossiped on, Lee recalled his life in the markets and wept with regret.

'Are you okay, Lee?' asked his friend; 'you look upset,' he exclaimed.

'It's just jet-lag,' he said, and the old boy accepted this excuse, never having flown and never likely to, either.

Lee now recalled how he came to work in the markets area, just after his escape from the orphanage. The first job he ever had, as a young teenager, was cleaning the massive sewers that ran under the village complex. When you opened the manholes the stench was overpowering, but once you climbed down the ladder you never noticed the smell as you chipped away at the rock hard build-up of effluent, which was blocking the tunnel. It was not a pleasant job, especially when the hard sewage broke loose and cascaded all over you, so Lee was really elated to be promoted some months later to the position of dog warden.

Huge metal dog-bins were situated all over town and used for collecting the actual dogs, but not their dirt or mess. If somebody reported a stray dog becoming a nuisance, Lee and his driver would entice the creature to one of the dog bins where a heavy blanket would be tossed over it, and the animal unceremoniously dumped into the huge metal container. As it landed on the others that had been surviving in the dark and heat without food or water, it would be set upon and have to fight for its life.

After some months Lee was given a job in the actual market as an apprentice, earning a decent wage, collecting the dogs from the bin-men and learning how to process them when they were left at the market.

When the bin-men brought the dogs to market there would be few survivors.

Only the strongest survived, by hobbling around on top of their dead comrades, guzzling what they could from their remains and sating their thirst by lapping up the blood of their dead companions.

Most of the animals were actually starving to death, because, once caught, they were never fed or watered for everyone knew they were destined for slaughter.

When they arrived in the market, the survivors were each placed in separate metal cages with wire-mesh floors. This made the animals easier to shift about and was perversely practical because the dogs often snared their paws in the mesh floors, making them easy prey for the handlers, who would later extract them from their cages using a wire noose around their necks.

There was also less maintenance involved because blood and faeces simply drained through the wire-mesh floor, with just a daily hose-down being necessary for the morning markets. The dogs actually relished this cleaning procedure, as it was the only nourishment they received since capture. The market manager's rationale was; 'Why feed something that was supposed to feed him?' It just didn't make sense!

The animals were delivered daily on a small truck, when Lee would take note of how many had survived their ordeal, and how many had perished. The market was divided into sections; one for sales of live dogs and the other for pelts and furs. The dead beasts were later carted off and processed into animal feed. Nothing was wasted, for this was modern day China after all; being the most expansive and progressive economy around, growing faster in wealth and technology than anywhere else in the world.

In the markets Lee discovered that even little dogs were popular. They could be fashioned into gloves and collars, and even muffs for the sleeves of coats, while the remaining flesh could feed some poor wretch for a week. None of the traders bothered with mink farms any more, for when dog fur was treated and dyed few buyers could tell the difference and it could be sold for a fraction of the price.

Chen told him that the favourite dogs, these days, were the large St. Bernard breeds and many people had become wealthy by farming them on a commercial scale.

Their furs were very prized, for a small coat could be made from just one animal. The coats had to be removed intact of course; a skill that Lee had readily acquired. The dog would be strung up, with a noose on its tail, leaving the hind legs free to work on. He would start with four circular incisions, just next the paws, before drawing a sharp blade down each leg. He would carefully slice the tendons, before drawing the blade down the length of the creature's belly. He had to be careful to avoid damaging the arteries or jugular veins for that proved too messy and the animal died too quickly.

The idea was to keep the creature alive long enough for the meat to stay fresh and tender. Some foreign tourists were horrified at this spectacle but Lee couldn't understand why, because this custom is common practice in China, Vietnam and Korea.

Few folks in modern China had any qualms about eating dogs, for most people knew that in Malawi a favourite delicacy was skewered rat, barbecued to a nice crispy texture and garnished with bird droppings; by comparison eating dogs seemed civilised. They were also aware that people in Europe devoured millions of giant birds, at Christmas.

Chen then declared. 'Until recently, many tourists took photos and videos of us preparing our dogs, but we had to ban cameras when an organisation called 'Animal Saviours' put a video of the whole procedure on the internet, and it is still posted there, so I have to be careful.'

'Why are you so worried, out here in the middle of nowhere?' queried Lee.

'Since you left here, Lee, small groups of animal lovers have formed, because some dogs are now kept as pets, as a status symbol, and some people even house filthy pot-bellied pigs from Vietnam. These fools often come here to protest, but because my picture is not on any videos I have not become a target so far, thank God.' Lee figured that God didn't come into the equation in this hellhole.

He recalled how the buyers always insisted their dogs be beaten to death, for the flesh would then taste better, being saturated with adrenalin and cholesterol. He started to recall how noisy and dangerous the whole procedure was, for sometimes even when a dog looked dead, he would unhook it, only to be bitten as it fell to the ground after being skinned. This was a messy routine, which he never got used to, for after the cuts to the paws were made, the metal muzzle was taken off. He would then grab the ends of the skin in each hand, near where the ankles were severed, and in one steady flourish pull the complete pelt in one piece from the rear legs right down over the snout, leaving only the eyelashes intact.

The creature would be hanging at eye level, so would ease the whole process as it started to convulse in agony, assisting the procedure as it writhed about, ripping its skin away from its own flesh.

Everyone would then savour the sweet smell of barbecued meat as a blowtorch was played over the bleeding carcass, to stem the blood flow, after which the pelt was taken to the fur traders ready for cleaning and dyeing.

The writhing animal was then cut down to hit the ground with only its eyebrows and tufts of ankle-fur left intact. As it rolled in the dirt not knowing why it was being punished, it acquired the characteristic of a new coat, as grit and soil clung to its raw flesh. What was left of its eyelids would cake up, rendering it virtually blind, but providing the opportunity for the stricken animal to be completely hosed down, before being slowly and methodically battered to death with baseball bats.

Its companions waiting in nearby cages would echo their serenade of anguish, sensing similar fates. Most of the creatures had painful festering wounds, which never healed in the heat of the metal containers. Even Lee found the noise and the smell overpowering and he never got used to the swarms of flies, relishing the odour of death.

The buyers would watch to check if the animal was still alive or if its eyes had glazed over, in death. Some came close up to inspect it and sometimes the poor dog, or what was left of it, would attempt to lick their hand; perhaps in amends for some imagined wrong, or as a gesture of hope, but these efforts were met with derision by the nouveau-riche buyers, who would giggle at this pathetic gesture. They realised their servants back home would soon be treating them to some succulent portion of this self-same dog, now convulsing in its death-throes, weeping blood in front of their pitiless gaze.

Lee choked with remorse when he recalled how he once carted these dogs on a trolley to the meat section of the market, only to have them suspended by nooses, skinned alive and beaten to death.

Some buyers would try and befriend him, for the success of their dinner parties depended greatly on his choice of dog, as there was a subtle difference in flavour between the breeds.

Those who came for furs would trust him to pick a beast with few bite and claw marks, for a clever buyer could purchase a decent dog only to have it skinned by Lee, and then sell the pelt elsewhere, thus purchasing the meat for a pittance. This was because the market traders were mostly regulars who would bribe Lee with offers of a sumptuous meal in their ornate mansions, on the pretext his services would be required, to prepare the feast.

Indeed … Lee was very aware that the regulars would have acquired many choice furs, which they would stash away, but needed him to keep a future eye out for matching pelts.

Lee spoke again to Chen, who told him, 'I've just returned from the 2016 dog-meat festival in Yulin, up north. I go every year for a week's work, skinning the dogs and cats. I made even more money than last year, for we had ten-thousand beasts there, and hundreds of thousands of customers. Did you know, Lee, that it only started in twenty-ten, but is now world-famous?'

'Is that still going?' queried Lee. 'I thought it would have collapsed by now, because of all the international protests?'

'No, my friend, business is better than ever, for we skin and cook right in front of the crowds, who get to taste the meat when it's really fresh and tasty.'

Lee said goodbye to his old friend, Chen, and wandered off to see if the ancient food-stall, where he used to eat was still functioning. He was surprised to see nothing had changed, so he indulged in some special noodles, declining the shark-fin soup, on offer.

He returned to his motel, changed into his suit, and picked up his car from the garage. He had decided to drive back to the markets to show Chen how prosperous he had become. When he drew up at the old man's workstation he was surprised to see his Mercedes was not the only one parked outside. As he went in, the old man introduced him to Madame Zsa-Zsa, who remembered Lee from years ago.

'Lee Fong!' she shouted, 'is that you? You look amazing. Is that your lovely car outside? I think it's the same model as mine.'

Lee confirmed her assumptions and enquired how her family was keeping.

'You remember Amy? She'll be back in a minute; you must say hallo,' cried Zsa-Zsa. 'She's quite famous now and more beautiful than ever.'

As Lee slowly sipped his cup of green tea he enquired why Zsa-Zsa was visiting the market.

'We have a dinner party this evening, to celebrate the release of Amy's latest movie. It's her first leading role in a Kung-Fu movie, and she plays the heroine, so we must celebrate. Why don't you join us, Lee, if you're not too busy?'

Lee agreed, for he was stunned when Amy Sang hovered into view. She was taller than he remembered but also more attractive, with thick long hair cascading around her flawless make-up. She recognised him immediately.

'Ah, ... so ... Lee Fong, my long lost love,' she cried out, seeming much more affectionate than when they last met. 'You look good,' she exclaimed. 'Good enough to eat,' she laughed, 'but I've just ordered a St. Bernard. Come and have a look at him?'

Lee went round the back to where a huge dog with a magnificent coat lay asleep in the sun. 'You didn't get *him* from the bin-men, did you?' he asked.

'Of course not ... he's from one of the breeders.'

She added. 'We want the best for our celebrity guests tonight.'

Zsa-Zsa interrupted, 'I've asked Lee to come along for old times' sake.'

'Of course, that would be wonderful. It'll be nice to see more of you,' said Amy, with a grin.

'And maybe you can prepare the dog for us,' said Zsa-Zsa.

'Only if you can change a load of American dollars for me,' declared Lee.

'Of course, darling,' Zsa-Zsa replied, 'but it would have to be a large amount, for our four guests tonight are all movie-moguls and none of them would consider anything less than ten thousand U.S.'

'Well,' said Lee, 'if I bring that amount for each of them, can you arrange it?'

'No problem, as long as you don't leave me out, for you know how welcome Yankee dollars are in China, and I will fix it so that you get the best black-market rate from all of us.'

After Lee assured her he would have the money available Zsa-Zsa and Amy seemed to garner even more respect and affection for him, but Lee had already decided his real motive in attending would be to rescue the St. Bernard, for he knew Zsa-Zsa wanted him to prepare this dog for her feast at the mansion.

They were conversing beside the dog when Lee lent over and patted its head.

'Do be careful, Lee,' said Amy, 'he might bite.' But, as she spoke the dog started to lick Lee's hand, and he decided he would free this lovely creature the first chance he got.

CHAPTER SEVENTEEN

When Lee returned home he showered, and changed into the dinner jacket he had hired for the occasion. In the past he had prepared many feasts for Madame Zsa-Zsa, so he knew the layout of the house and the kitchens.

When he arrived the dog was already tethered in the garage, so he parked his Mercedes outside and lowered the roof. He reclined the passenger seat in the hope he could bundle the huge dog into the car and escape with it. When he entered the lavish dining room, Zsa-Zsa informed him that a special hors d-oeuvres would be served her special guests, before the main course.

Addressing Amy, she said, 'why not give Lee the grand tour and don't forget the master bedroom.' This comment seemed to draw a few sniggers from the other guests, but Lee never noticed, for he was preoccupied with plans for freeing the dog.

But he followed Amy around the house, as she showed him the various en-suite bedrooms and the Sauna and the Jacuzzi. He was entranced by how beautiful she looked and felt intoxicated by the scent of her exotic perfume.

She led him into the largest bedroom and declared, 'This is my room, totally private, so I do what I like in here.'

She signalled intent by locking the door behind her and staring straight into his eyes. Lee had not been in a woman's presence since Lucy, and just being near Amy made him rampant with desire. She was dressed in a shiny silk sarong, which clung to her every curve, and Lee became fascinated, watching her easy grace as she strutted round in vertiginous heels, echoing the allure of her long legs. Before he knew what was happening, she was grasping him in a passionate embrace.

They were soon entwined on the huge circular waterbed where he humbled himself to her beauty, feeling enraptured by her sublime sexuality, as she responded to his deepest desires. He was beguiled by the way her long silken hair cascaded round her breasts to flow in luxurious abundance down her back, caressing the confines of an elegant waist. He surrendered himself to her expertise, indulging her carnal hunger as she spurred his emotions to a fever pitch.

She confused and abused him, as he wallowed in the control she wielded, which contrasted so starkly with the innocence of his previous loves. He found in her a vibrant sensual woman, revelling in the supreme art of her eroticism. She finally took him to a point where pain blurred into pleasure, as intoxicating desires fired his imagination to virgin heights.

She immersed him in a surreal euphoric world, where a tsunami of emotions flooded his very soul, creating new summits of pleasure. All fear and frustration left Lee's troubled mind, as they consumed each other in tumultuous embrace.

Afterwards, he felt strangely revived with a new perspective on life, because this absorption with Amy had granted him a new peace, where memories of the past seemed to evaporate like the sweat on his brow. In the silence of the night, he realised the palette of his mind would be forever etched with the memory of their indulgence.

In eloquent silence they slowly dressed and made their way down stairs.

As they entered the drawing room, a giant television screen was flickering in the background, and suddenly the guests all erupted in a chorus of applause.

Lee had no idea why they were clapping, until Madame Zsa-Zsa declared, 'Lee, my boy, you have done us proud!' It was only then that he saw what the others were watching. It was a blow-by-blow recording of his encounter with Amy, and he suddenly realised that he had been set up as the evening's cabaret act.

Zsa-Zsa then haughtily declared. 'Perhaps I should have told you, Lee, ... Amy only got into movies because she made so many great porn-videos for the internet. These still bring in lots of revenue, and we are all so grateful for your contribution, Lee ... Congratulations! You will now be starring in one of your own, which will soon be posted all over the world.'

Lee felt sick to his stomach; he had defied and denied not only Tom's advice, but also the warnings of the old boy in the park - and the monk in the monastery. He now felt he had betrayed *three* people and realised he had just fallen foul to the pernicious practice they had all warned him about. He was no longer an innocent victim, but an active participant in this abhorrent activity!

He stared at Amy, but she was obviously wise to the game, for she spurned his glance, ignoring him for the rest of the evening.

Zsa-Zsa gave him a stiff drink and presented him with all the money she had collected from the guests. It came to five-hundred-thousand Chinese Yuan.

She then arrogantly informed Lee it was time for him to go and prepare the dog as the rest of the company were about to have their 'special treat'. He was glad not to be included, as he just wished to be on his own. He was so ashamed and disappointed he felt almost suicidal.

As he retired to the garage to get the dog, he noticed two white-coated chefs going downstairs to the wine cellars.

He glanced into the dining-room and saw a large round glass table with a circular hole cut in the middle. There were six place settings around the table, each with a small plate and a carefully positioned silver spoon.

His curiosity heightened when he heard squeals coming from the cellar, and watched with alarm as a large monkey was pulled up the stairs and into the room. The chefs had four strong straps attached to its arms and legs, which they now used to tether the creature under the table, so that only the top of its head protruded through the centre of the glass table.

One of the chefs returned with tiny ornate bowls which he gently placed on the plates, warning the guests to be careful, as they were very hot. The other chef entered the room with a battery-powered gadget to which a small circular blade was attached. The monkey was visible to the diners but could only guess what was happening, as its head was muzzled and totally immobile.

As the chef switched on the gadget, its small circular blade spun at high speed. He placed the saw squarely on the table, and proceeded to rotate it around the captive's skull. The device cut in with ruthless efficiency, as the animal spat out in pain and rage.

When the chef had sawn around the skull, his assistant, with a deft twist, quickly removed the top of it. The severed part came away cleanly, with just a little blood dripping onto the glass table, which was quickly mopped up to provide the guests a clear view of their captive. The creature's grey pulsing brain was now exposed - and Lee froze in horror.

It was generally assumed this practice had died out but Lee knew that some nouveau-rich were still convinced live monkey brains were a potent aphrodisiac. A cheer arose as the other chef popped some champagne corks, and filled their glasses, as the guests grasped the long silver spoons.

As the chefs left the room, Madame Zsa-Zsa leaned over with her own spoon and carefully scooped a small portion of live brain. She paused to smell its aroma, like a fine wine, and delicately tasted its contents. Slowly licking her lips, she nodded approval to the other guests, who then rose in turn to gather their portions of live brain, slowly consuming them with sips of champagne.

The creature had stopped grunting and growling by the time the six guests had filled their bowls. It was steadily losing all its faculties as the silver spoons dug deeper. Its responses now slowed from spitting and hissing to feeble spasmodic jerks as all life was being steadily drawn from its limp body.

As guest of honour, Amy Sang was called upon to drain the last succulent remnants from the skull. The guests paused to observe as she hovered sensuously over the creature, pouting coldly into its bright brown eyes, now blazing with anger; these slowly glazed into a dull lifeless grey as she methodically scooped the last vestiges of life from the helpless creature. A round of applause greeted this coup-de-grace, whereupon Amy Sang performed a graceful curtsy.

Lee was stunned by the callous manner with which Amy had treated him, but he was more shocked and incensed by her treatment of this helpless animal, and sadly recalled what the old man had told him ... 'Femininity is no criterion for compassion.' He decided it was now time for payback.

He went out and secured the dog in his car, with its leash wrapped around the passenger door-handle. He gathered his money together and placed it in the centre-console of the Mercedes. He knew the dog would keep anyone away from the car, so he started the engine and ran into the enormous kitchen to where the large ovens were situated. He had spotted some very large canisters of propane waiting to be loaded into Madame's motorhome and he managed to lift these directly onto the oven rings, which he then turned on at full blast. The wine and champagne were flowing, and the chefs had gone home. Everyone thought Lee was in the kitchens, preparing the dog for the main course so nobody was aware of his car starting up, with the St. Bernard sitting in the passenger seat.

As soon as he had placed the huge canisters on the gas rings he walked briskly into the dining room.

'Sorry, I'm leaving. I can't do this anymore; there are too many animals in this place.'

Zsa-Zsa, humouring him, declared. 'We will get you some help, Lee. You need a servant,' she laughed. 'You're quickly going up in the world.'

'Not as quick as you,' shouted Lee, as he turned and bolted for his car. As he roared up the driveway he felt the blast of heat, as a huge fireball engulfed the whole mansion. Lee knew from experience that nobody would get out alive, but also realised he would now be a fugitive in his own land. Driving to his motel as fast as he dared, he dashed inside to pick up his passport and credit cards. He figured he was going to need them very soon. He decided to head for the Vietnamese border, which was a ten-hour drive away, where his money could buy him all the security he needed. He figured he could also sell the car on the black market for a good price. He drove all through the night, only stopping once to buy petrol, and food for the dog, which he found to be great company. He hoped that the proprietor hadn't noticed his nervousness, as he paid for the fuel using one of his credit cards for the first time. This was a huge mistake for the garage monitored all such transactions.

Lee sensed the dog would protect him as he had protected it. He was just cruising along, in the light of a new dawn, when he saw the flashing lights of police vehicles in his rear view mirror. He also heard the throbbing of a helicopter overhead and realised the game was up.

He drove like a madman but found he couldn't lose the convoy of police, as they were more familiar with the local terrain. Suddenly, a flash of inspiration made him open the centre-console which held all the money. He grabbed huge handfuls of the stuff and proceeded to fling it out the open roof, watching in amazement as the massive flurry of notes caused the convey to skid to a halt, as everybody rushed to grasp whatever they could lay their hands on.

This diversion gave Lee a chance to escape but as he drove towards a river bridge, on the border crossing, he tensed up as he realised it was blocked by a wedge of police cars. He knew now there was no escape and realised that with all the witnesses in the markets he would definitely be convicted for the fire and for the murder of some very prominent citizens. In China murder means the death sentence, so he made a spontaneous decision to sacrifice himself in a blaze of glory, by ramming into the string of cars across the bridge.

Then he heard the whine of the dog and decided that even if he didn't deserve to live … at least the dog did.

He couldn't bear to sacrifice it, so braked to a sudden halt. The dog could smell the tension in the air and sensed that this was goodbye. As Lee bent forward to open the car door it nuzzled his face and gently nibbled his ear, as if to say goodbye; then it jumped out, just as the police were closing in on him.

As he was being handcuffed, he saw the huge dog bounding off, down the banks of the river. The cops had their man and weren't interested in a stupid dog. It was now free but Lee was behind bars within the hour.

The court case was a hurried affair, because sordid details of the celebrities' perverted pursuits were beginning to leak out.

Lee was sentenced to death by firing squad, on multiple counts of homicide, and taken to the prison where his execution would take place.

After some days chained in a dank cell, immersed in total darkness, he lost all track of time.

One evening, as he was being given his last meal, they informed him that he would later be taken to the prison courtyard, to be shot at dawn.

He knew the execution system was always the same in China and Malaysia. Two heavy machine guns rigged in tandem, were fired electrically from some remote guardhouse.

Later that evening he was transferred to another cell, next to the guardhouse, for his last night on Earth. At least this cell had a small window, through which he could see a tree on the hill, just overlooking the prison.

For hours he stared intently at the beauty of the heavens, drinking in the relentless beauty of the stars, and gazing into the cold wilderness of the courtyard. For the first time in his life, he wanted to stay awake all night, as he listened quietly to the guards gambling over the credit cards they had taken from his wallet.

As the first light of dawn illuminated the horizon, Lee Fong Chu was marched to the far end of an enclosed courtyard and shackled to a large wooden gantry, in the form of a cross. The guards had confiscated his shirt and his shoes, and as they frogmarched him across the barren courtyard the damp soil gathered between his toes. He had some cuts to his feet, but at this stage wasn't worrying about any infection.

But he did wonder whether Mother Earth, which he now viewed as a living breathing organism, might someday retaliate if mankind kept on abusing her; whether she might begin to view humanity as a virus intent on her destruction. He imagined her conjuring up some final apocalyptic plague, to rid herself of the infection of man; erasing all these creatures that were slowly destroying her.

His outright arms were now strapped to the top of a horizontal crossbar, and his feet bound to the bottom upright.

The guards had retreated to the hut from where they would fire the guns. Two guns were used, in case one jammed. The high-walled courtyard was now empty as Lee stared into the muzzles of the high-velocity guns mounted on solid tripods and zeroed directly towards him.

'So it's time,' he thought. 'I don't know where I'm going, but it must be to a better place, something more than this; a better world.'

As he focused on the stars, realizing he would never see them again, he wondered if there were other planets out there, where other individuals hung on other crosses, awaiting death.

Lee stared at the blizzard of stars, now rapidly fading in the early morning sun, as it split the horizon. He now felt he was seeing it for the first time, in the same spectacular fashion that he had sensed so deeply on his psychedelic trip in the park, with Lucy.

But never before had he noticed the stark beauty of a sunrise; or drunk so deeply of its radiance.

As he felt its warm glow on his cold face, a new light entered his world and in an instant everything made sense. He sensed the soft earth beneath his feet and reflected that the soil itself had given mankind all the materials and minerals necessary to construct everything on the planet. He now wondered at the tree outside his cell window, and marvelled at the way it could flourish and grow, to expand its limbs ever outwards, nourishing the very air he breathed.

He remembered Tom telling him about the enormity of the universe and suddenly, ... Lee recalled Tom telling him that many people believed that if there was no God, man would need to invent one!

Lee now realised that Tom's statement implied that man needs God, and conversely, that God needs man. Then he realised that God would never actually need anything or anybody; but may simply want humankind, as His creation. For why would some omnipotent power just float around for all eternity without creating something: and would what it created not be something which it could cherish and love? And would such a power not find its own existence an exercise in futility, unless its omnipotence could be utilised at some point in time.

He now decided. - Yes, of course ... there must be a God.

He realised everything was just too complicated to be any other way. His whole life was bound in bitterness; he had tasted pain and loss ... yes; but also love and compassion. He had discovered that possessions do not provide happiness and that money cannot purchase real love; but here was another reality: he now knew that if you live by the sword, you die by the sword.

Deep within him he felt a spark of remorse stirring. Embers of shame and sorrow now surfaced in a sea of guilt, as he recalled his evil deeds. As flames of truth now clutched at his soul he recalled La-Lu's faith and devotion, and suddenly realised just how much she really loved him. Seeds of remorse now ignited his conscience and he felt deeply sorry and ashamed for all his stupidity.

Sensing that he only had moments left to make his peace with the world and the God he would soon meet, he closed his eyes for the last time. Lee had always dreaded dying alone, but now realised that death is the one thing we must all face on our own. He resolved that whenever he did meet this God, he would tell Him just how sorry he was, for all the sufferings he had inflicted on his fellow beings. As he awaited death, he felt a strange metallic taste in his mouth - but memories from the orphanage told him exactly what this was. It was the raw taste of fear, but he felt it for only a moment - the very moment that he died - when the twin guns erupted in a ferocious blaze of fire.

Lee was instantly oblivious to their super-sonic shells striking his body, for there was no time for any pain to register. Neither was he conscious of their noise, because death itself immersed him before their thunder had a chance to reach and surround his soul.

In a faraway land, on the other side of the world, a tall nun stood alone in another walled courtyard. She was pensively watching the same sun - now setting - on a different horizon. She had paused in her meditation as she clutched a large crucifix to her bosom. Staring out at the darkening sky, she felt a sudden shiver, as a cold chill ran down her spine. Outside in the distance, a dog began to howl.

AUTHORS PAGE

This book, and others written by the author, may be ordered directly from authorhouse.co.uk or from major booksellers, or Amazon, for under £10, but may be purchased in bulk from the Author for half-price, and can even be downloaded, for free, from his website, which is …

Radical Rooney.com

They include

'The Century Collection' 'A Year on the Streets'
'For the Love of Dog' 'A Survivor's Story'
'Tall Tales and Short Stories'
e-mail radicalrooney@hotmail.com
Landline +44-28-90-60-48-33

20900322R00166

Printed in Great Britain
by Amazon